"What aren't you t[...]

Westley's question jerked Felicity's gaze to meet his intense stare. She felt her heart pound as her instincts warred with Ian's directive.

"Felicity, I can't protect you if I don't know what is going on."

True. Westley was the only one standing between her and a potential killer.

Two killers, in fact.

And if Westley didn't know there was more than one threat out there, then how effective could he be?

She inhaled, blew out the breath and said, "My father's death wasn't an accident."

* * *

Books by Terri Reed

Love Inspired Suspense

Military K-9 Unit

Mission to Protect

Classified K-9 Unit

Guardian
Classified K-9 Unit Christmas
"Yuletide Stalking"

Northern Border Patrol

Danger at the Border
Joint Investigation
Murder Under the Mistletoe
Ransom
Identity Unknown

Visit the Author Profile page at Harlequin.com for more titles.

MISSION TO PROTECT

TERRI REED

HARLEQUIN® LOVE INSPIRED® SUSPENSE

Special thanks and acknowledgment are given to Terri Reed for her contribution to the Military K-9 Unit miniseries.

Recycling programs
for this product may
not exist in your area.

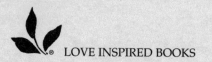

LOVE INSPIRED BOOKS

ISBN-13: 978-1-335-49028-5

Mission to Protect

Copyright © 2018 by Harlequin Books S.A.

www.Harlequin.com

Printed in U.S.A.

Search me, O God, and know my heart:
try me, and know my thoughts:
And see if there be any wicked way in me,
and lead me in the way everlasting.
—Psalms 139:23-24

This book is dedicated to the Military Working Dogs and the service women and men who defend our country.

Thank you to my editors, Tina James and Emily Rodmell, for including me in this series and for your support and patience. Thank you to the other authors who gave me so much encouragement during a difficult time. Thank you to Leah Vale for your never-ending friendship. And thank you to my family for your unconditional love.

ONE

The back door of Canyon Air Force Base's military working-dog training facility stood open. It should have been closed and locked tight.

Alarm slithered through lead trainer Master Sergeant Westley James like the venomous red, yellow and black coral snake inhabiting this part of Texas.

Something was wrong.

As he entered the building an eerie chill went down his neck that had nothing to do with the April early-morning air. The stillness echoed through the center as loud as a jet taking off. His pulse spiked. He rushed to the kennel room and drew up short.

The kennels were empty. All of them.

Lying on the floor in a pool of blood were the two night-shift dog trainers, Airman Tamara Peterson and Airman Landon Martelli. Each had been shot in the chest.

Grief clutched at Westley's heart. Careful not to disturb the scene, he checked for pulses. None.

They had both been murdered.

Under the left arms of Tamara and Landon were a

red rose and a folded white note, the calling card of a notorious serial killer.

Horror slammed into him. The news report he'd heard this morning on his way to work had become reality.

Boyd Sullivan, aka the Red Rose Killer, had escaped prison and was back on base.

Staff Sergeant Felicity Monroe jerked awake to the fading sound of her own scream echoing in her head. Sweat drenched her nightshirt. The pounding of her heart hurt in her chest, making bile rise to burn her throat. Darkness surrounded her.

Where was she? Fear locked on to her like a guided missile and wouldn't let go. Panic fluttered at the edge of her mind.

Memories flooded her system.

Her father!

A sob tore from her throat.

The familiar scent of jasmine from the bouquet of flowers on her bedside table grounded her. She was in her bedroom of the house on Canyon Air Force Base in southwest Texas. The home she'd shared with her father before his accidental death a month ago.

Her breathing slowed. She wiped at the wet tears on her cheeks and shook away the fear and panic.

Just a nightmare. One in a long string of them.

According to Dr. Flintman, the base therapist, she suffered mild post-traumatic stress disorder from finding her father after his fall from a ladder he had climbed to clean the gutters on the house. Knowing why her brain was doing this didn't make the images seared in her mind any less upsetting.

She filled her lungs with several deep breaths and sought the clock across the room on the dresser.

The clock's red glow was blocked by the silhouette of a person looming at the end of her bed.

Was her mind playing a trick on her again? Or was she still stuck in her nightmare? She blinked rapidly to clear the sleep from her eyes.

Her breath caught and held.

No trick.

Someone was in her room.

Full-fledged panic jackknifed through her, jolting her system into action. Self-preservation kicked in. She rolled to the side of the bed and landed soundlessly on the floor. With one hand, she reached for the switch of the bedside-table lamp, while her other hand searched for the baseball bat she kept under the bed.

Holding the bat up with her right hand, she flicked on the light. A warm glow dispelled the shadows and revealed she was alone. Or was she?

With bat in hand, she went through the house, turning on every light. No one was there.

She frowned and worked to calm her racing pulse.

This wasn't the first time she'd thought someone had been in the house.

But this time had seemed so real.

Back in her bedroom, she looked again at the clock. Wait a minute. It was turned to face the wall. A shiver of unease wracked her body. The red numbers had been facing the bed when she'd retired last night. She was convinced of it.

And her dresser drawers were slightly open. She peeked inside. Her clothes were mussed, as if someone had rummaged through them. She wasn't a neat freak or anything, but her military training and her air force father had taught her to keep her things in proper order.

What was going on?

Was the stress and grief of her father's passing messing with her brain, as her therapist suggested? Was she losing her mind?

Wouldn't that just be the icing on the cake? Her mother already thought she was nuts for choosing to join the United States Air Force and train military dogs for service rather than follow in her footsteps and pursue a high-powered career in corporate law.

Felicity set aside the baseball bat.

Maybe someone was pulling a joke on her.

She dismissed the idea quickly. She didn't know anyone that cruel.

She turned the clock to see the time. Five after five in the morning. Perfect. The one day she could sleep in, and her psyche wouldn't let her. She wasn't expected at the training center until tonight. She usually had Sundays off and worked the Saturday-night shift, but had traded with Airman Tamara Peterson, who was taking a few days of leave to visit her parents and wanted to head out Sunday morning.

Felicity glanced at the clock again. Maybe she could nap for an hour or so more, then go to church.

Noises outside the bedroom window startled her. It was too early for most people to be up on a Sunday morning. She pushed aside the room-darkening curtain. The first faint rays of sunlight marched over the Texas horizon with hues of gold, orange and pink.

They provided enough light for Felicity to see a parade of dogs running loose along Base Boulevard. It could only be the dogs from the K-9 training center.

Stunned, her stomach clenched.

Someone had literally let the dogs out. Most of them, by the looks of it. At least a hundred or more canines filled the street and were quickly leaving the area.

Felicity's chest constricted. Had Tamara or Landon, the other trainer on last night's shift, forgotten to lock the gate? That didn't seem likely. Both were experienced trainers. Uneasy dread gripped her by the throat.

A dog barked, reminding her that the canines needed to be rounded up and returned to their kennels. She didn't want any of them to get hurt. Some of the dogs suffered PTSD from their service, while others were being trained to serve. Many were finished with their training and ready to be partnered, but set loose like this...

Galvanized into action, she hastily dressed in her battle-ready uniform.

On the way out the door, she grabbed her cell phone, intending to call her boss, Master Sergeant Westley James. Before she could dial, her phone pinged with an incoming alert text from the training center.

Urgent. Dogs' kennels tampered with. Red Rose Killer escaped prison and believed to be on base. Use caution. Report in ASAP.

Felicity stopped in her tracks. Her heart fell to her feet then bounced back into her throat as fear struck hard through her core.

The Red Rose Killer.

Boyd Sullivan. Cold eyes, merciless.

She shuddered.

Two years ago, after being dishonorably discharged

from the air force during basic training, Boyd had returned to his hometown of Dill, Texas, and killed five people whom he'd believed had wronged him in some way.

The media had dubbed him the Red Rose Killer because he would leave a red rose and a note for his intended victims, taunting them with the warning—*I'm coming for you*. Then he made good on his threat, and each victim was found with an additional red rose and a new note tucked under their arm, with the words *Got you*.

A Dill sheriff's deputy and her K-9 partner had been the ones to bring down Sullivan. He'd been captured, convicted and sent to prison.

And now he'd escaped and was on base.

Why would he release the dogs? She remembered he always liked the furry creatures.

She dialed Westley's cell.

He answered on the first ring. "Felicity. Did you hear the news?"

"Yes. There are dogs everywhere in base housing," she told him.

"They are everywhere on base period." His voice sounded extra grim. "We need to bring them in."

"I'll retrieve as many as I can here and bring them over to the kennels."

"Good. I'll send others over to help." There was a pause then he said, "I should tell you there have been two murders."

She stilled. Fear whispered down her spine. Her pulse spiked. "Murders?" She swayed. *Please, Lord, no.* "Tamara? Landon?"

"Yes."

Her heart sank. Tears flooded her eyes. That explained why the dogs were loose. She knew neither trainer would be so careless. "Did Boyd Sullivan kill them?

"That's the assumption. Each was found with a red rose tucked under their arm and a note that read, 'Got you.'"

"Boyd used that same tactic in Dill. But why would he go after Tamara and Landon?"

"I don't know," Westley replied. "But right now the dogs need us."

Westley's no-nonsense tone made her pull herself together. The last thing she wanted was for him to consider her weak. He was stingy enough with his praise, especially for her. He was always watching and waiting for her to mess up, but just because she was the newest member, and the youngest on his team, didn't mean she didn't belong.

Strangely, though, she didn't feel the familiar prickling at the back of her neck that his words normally brought.

Her usual irritation with her handsome boss was muffled by grief and the need to act. This time he was correct. The dogs needed her.

She wiped at the tears falling down her cheeks and took a shuddering breath. "Of course. I'm going to find our dogs."

"Be careful. Boyd is still out there."

His husky tone sent little shivers over her skin. She frowned, annoyed by her reaction. Though his words expressed concern for her, she knew his real concern was for the dogs. She could only imagine his upset. The dogs were his life.

Had Westley been the one to find Tamara Peterson and Landon Martelli? How had they been killed? Who would tell their families? Had they suffered? A million questions ran through her head, but she forced herself to stay focused. To be strong. Her mother would be proud of her. Maybe. "I'll be careful," she assured him and hung up.

After pocketing her phone, she dug through her satchel for a small canister of pepper spray and slipped it into her front pocket. In case she met Boyd along the way.

Master Sergeant Westley James paced by the back wall of the large auditorium-style conference room.

Shortly after discovering the bodies of his trainers and alerting the base's USAF Security Forces, Westley had received a call from the base commander to report here. His stomach twisted with grief and shock as he glanced around the room, noting an eclectic mix of high-ranking officers and civilian personnel. With over seven thousand people on base, keeping Canyon Air Force Base running took a large staff.

He couldn't sit, though most everyone else had taken a seat. His heart still beat too fast. This wasn't where he should be. He needed to be out searching for the dogs. He struggled to stay in the moment.

The base commander's executive assistant, a civilian, Brenda Blakenship, had come in a few moments ago to say the debriefing would begin when the base commander and the basic-training commander arrived. Then she'd left again. Conversations in hushed tones were a reflection of the somber mood.

As the lead trainer of the military working dogs

training center, Westley oversaw the welfare of the two hundred and fifty dogs currently being trained in multiple disciplines from explosives and electronic detection to patrol. He was also responsible for the trainers and the various handlers from different branches of the military. It was a challenging post. He loved it.

And now the lives of two of his trainers had been senselessly taken, and the dogs were wandering the base, putting them in jeopardy. He itched to be out there looking for the dogs. Many of them were traumatized from combat service, which would make retrieving them that much harder. If the dogs were approached by someone they didn't know and trust… He feared for the safety of both dogs and humans.

Could this day get any worse?

His phone buzzed with an incoming text. He glanced at the message from Master Sergeant Caleb Streeter, another trainer, and was gratified to read the number of dogs brought safely in by the training staff. But there were still many left to recover.

The door to the auditorium opened. Westley put away his phone as Brenda entered with a folder in her hand and a grim expression on her face. Behind her, the base commander, Lieutenant General Hall, strode into the conference room, his face ashen.

"I've just received word that Chief Master Sergeant Clint Lockwood was found dead in his home of a gunshot wound to the heart," Lieutenant General Hall stated flatly. "A red rose and note were also found."

Shock rippled through the room.

Westley placed a hand on the wall to steady himself. The horror of finding the two trainers' bodies was still etched in Westley's brain. And now to hear that Lockwood was gone as well…

Lord, why would You allow this?

Westley didn't hold his breath waiting on God to give him an answer. Westley was used to God's silence. As a scared kid hiding from the constant chaos of his parents' fighting, he'd often asked God to make them stop. But the fighting never did. Not until his dad was incarcerated, which threw Westley into a different sort of chaos.

Questions came at the base commander with lightning speed from those seated around the room.

"Has the weapon been found?" the air force recruitment commander asked from his seat at the front of the room.

"Have we locked down the base?" the chief master sergeant of the 12th flying training wing called out.

"Have the FBI, OSI and the local police been notified?" the cyberspace operations commander asked.

"How did Boyd Sullivan escape prison?" the vice commander of the medical wing demanded to know.

Lieutenant General Hall raised a hand to silence the group. "Please, I will answer your questions as best I can. The weapon has not been found. The base is on lockdown. The feds and the local law enforcement will work closely with both Security Forces and the Office of Special Investigations." A fierce light entered the Lieutenant General's gaze. "Our problem is not how Boyd Sullivan escaped prison, but how he got on base."

"Is he targeting those who were in his basic military training?" Security Forces Captain Justin Blackwood asked.

"He must have had help," the commander of the airlift wing pointed out.

Lieutenant General Hall once again raised his hand and the room quieted. "If he holds true to form, he will most likely go after anyone he deems has wronged him. No doubt Sullivan blamed Chief Master Sergeant Lockwood for the dishonorable discharge."

Westley's fingers curled into fists at his sides. Boyd would pay dearly for his evil deeds. Westley prayed no other lives would be taken by Boyd's hand.

"We must consider Sullivan will go after those in his basic military training." Lieutenant General Hall nodded at Brenda.

She opened the file folder in her hand. "I've compiled a list of the personnel currently on base who were in the same training class as Boyd Sullivan."

"Our first order of business is to secure these individuals and anyone else who had prior interaction with Boyd," Lieutenant General Hall interjected. "Then we will root out the person who has helped this predator get on base."

As Brenda read the names, Westley tried to remember if Tamara or Landon had been in Sullivan's BMT group, or even been on base at the time. He didn't think so.

"Staff Sergeant Felicity Monroe."

Hearing his trainer's name jerked Westley's thoughts back to the conference room. Felicity. His stomach dropped as his pulse spiked. She was supposed to have been on duty last night, but had changed shifts.

Had she been Sullivan's intended target?

Fear streaked through his system like a fighter jet heading to battle. He couldn't let another person for whom he was responsible die. Not on his watch. He had to protect her.

Without asking permission, Westley raced out of the auditorium. He had to find Felicity.

Felicity's search for the dogs wasn't going very well. With the base alive and on alert, the dogs sensed the anxiety rippling through the air and were skittish. She moved with a slow, easy gait so as not to spook two dogs in her sights, a three-year-old German shepherd named Tiger and a two-year-old Belgian Malinois named Riff. Both were sniffing around the commissary.

As she approached, both dogs lifted their heads to eye her, their tails swishing.

"Come," she commanded while holding a treat in her hand against her thigh, which would bring the dogs in close enough to grab by the collar.

Tiger abandoned his sniffing to comply. As he took the treat from her, she hooked her fingers beneath his collar and swiftly attached a leash to the ring. Now to get the Malinois.

"Riff," she said. "Here, boy."

The dog's ears twitched but he made no move to obey. She and Tiger stepped closer. Riff moved away, nose back to the ground. Frustration beat at her temples. "Come on, Riff."

The dog had done well inside the confines of the center, but out in the open, not so much. Now she understood why Westley had said the dog wasn't ready to be paired with a human. She'd disagreed at the time and had even accused him, albeit silently, of holding back Riff because he didn't like her. Now she knew her boss had been right.

Riff had a long way to go in his training. She didn't relish admitting that to Westley. He'd give her that tight-lipped nod that irritated her nerves and made her feel as if she didn't measure up to his standards. Her commanding officer certainly knew how to push her buttons…unfortunately.

Tiger spun around and barked, his tail rigid and his ears up.

Seconds later she heard the sound of pounding feet and her adrenaline spiked. She reached for her pepper spray with her free hand and whirled with the can up and her finger hovering over the trigger, ready to protect herself from an assault.

Westley held his hands up, palms facing out, as he skidded to a halt. "Whoa. It's me."

Not Boyd, as she dreaded. Heart racing, she lowered the canister, thankful she hadn't let loose a stream of stinging spray.

Tiger relaxed and moved closer to Westley.

Felicity took in a deep breath. Exasperation made her voice sharp when she said, "You scared me." Her gaze jumped to Riff as the dog ran away. "Riff!"

The dog disappeared around the corner of the building.

"You were right," she conceded. "We need to work on his recall."

"We will," Westley assured her as he took Tiger's lead from her hand. "Right now, my only concern is you."

The grim set of his jaw alerted her heightened senses. Had she done something wrong? Made a mistake? Her defenses rose, making her straighten. "Me? I'm doing my best to bring the dogs in."

For a moment, confusion entered his gaze then cleared. "Lieutenant General Hall believes Boyd Sullivan is targeting those who were in his basic-military-training class," he replied, his voice harsh.

She took a step back. The same alarm that had flooded her this morning, when she'd thought someone was standing at the foot of her bed, seeped through her now. Had it been Boyd? A shudder of revulsion worked over her flesh.

"But that doesn't make any sense," she said. At Westley's arched eyebrow, she added, "Neither Tamara nor Landon were in our group."

"Exactly," he said. "I think you were his intended target last night."

She sucked in a breath. Her lungs burned as his words sank in. She swallowed convulsively as her mouth dried from the terror that was already pumping in her blood. She shook her head. "You can't know that for sure."

Was she responsible for her friends' deaths?

A spasm of guilt and pain twisted her insides. She wanted to fall to her knees and ask God why, but with Westley standing there, she remained upright and silently sent up the question. *Why, Lord?*

"He also killed Chief Master Sergeant Lockwood."

The air swooshed out of her lungs. The basic military training commander. The one who'd kicked Boyd out of the air force. Felicity was friends with Maisy Lockwood, the chief master sergeant's daughter and a civilian preschool teacher.

Agitation revved through Felicity's system. She trembled with the restless urge to move. "I need to see Maisy. She must be devastated."

Westley nodded. "Seeing her will have to wait. We

need to take Tiger, here, to the training center then go find more dogs."

"We can put him in my backyard. I'll set out water on the back deck. He'll be fine there while we search."

He seemed to contemplate her suggestion. She gritted her teeth, expecting him to argue with her. He always thought his way was best, and because he was in charge that left little room for discussion. She prepared to defend her suggestion but he nodded, which surprised her. "That works."

Unsure what to make of Westley, she led the way down Base Boulevard to her house. Her gaze snagged on the black curbside mailbox. The drop-down door was propped half-open.

What was going on? It hadn't been open when she'd left the house earlier. Her steps faltered. Was her sanity really slipping?

Just this morning she'd imagined someone standing at the foot of her bed and now this? She didn't want to think about the other times when she'd had the feeling someone had been inside her home.

Maybe she needed to take up Dr. Flintman on his offer of medication to suppress her mild PTSD. She would have before except she didn't want to be medicated and give Westley any reason to wash her out of the training center. And she worried that would be a big one, given that he already had it in for her. From the day she stepped into the center, she'd had the feeling he wanted her gone.

"What's wrong?" The concern coating Westley's words shimmied down her spine.

For all his fault-finding with her, he was being a

supportive boss today. Unusual but appreciated. She needed to take a deep breath and gather herself together.

"Nothing, I hope." But she couldn't tear her gaze away from the mailbox. She stepped closer and she pushed the door, intending to close it, but something blocked it from shutting.

Aggravated, she yanked the door all the way open. A red rose popped out to lie flat on the open metal flap. She gasped and jerked her hand back as if the flower was a copperhead snake.

Then her eyes focused on a folded white sheet of paper.

Her knees threatened to give out. Boyd had been here.

One thing was clear—she hadn't been imagining things. Yet, her mind tapped with the niggling knowledge that strange things had been happening long before today. Her body went numb as fear drenched her in a cold sweat.

"We need to call Security Forces."

Westley's deep, gravelly voice rumbled in her chest. She could only nod. Her tongue stuck to the roof of her mouth.

After he made the call, he turned her to face him. "Look at me," he instructed.

She stared at him. Morning sunlight reflected in his light blue eyes and gleamed in his dark hair. She couldn't deny he was handsome, and at this moment, he, of all people, anchored her. If she wasn't so freaked out, she'd find that odd. She wasn't sure the man even liked her. But there was concern in his eyes now. Concern for her. Crazy, really. But then again, it had been that kind of morning.

She took a breath and then swallowed. "I think he may have been in my house."

"What?"

"When I woke up this morning someone stood at the foot of my bed. But when I turned on the light, no one was there." She didn't mention the other times she'd had the sensation that someone had been in her home or was watching her. Today was bad enough.

"Are you kidding me?" he sputtered. "Why didn't you report it?"

She bristled at the censure in his tone. "I thought I was imagining things." Her heart beat painfully in her chest. She yanked her gaze from him and stared at the house. "But why leave a note and the rose when he could have killed me in my sleep?"

Westley studied her face, making her want to squirm. "Could it have been a nightmare?"

The sympathy and understanding in his tone sent another rush of anxiety through her. Did he suspect her PTSD? Had Dr. Flintman talked to her boss? The thought horrified her.

"Maybe," she admitted, not willing to fully commit to the diagnosis and what that might mean for her future with the K-9 unit.

"You've suffered a tragic loss recently," he reminded her more gently than she would have thought him capable, making her wonder if he'd suffered the loss of someone close to him as well.

Losing her father to a senseless accident was a scar she'd carry with her forever. And it may be the cause of her imaginings, yet… "It doesn't make sense," she said again.

"What doesn't?"

Would Westley think she was going nuts? She was loath to give him any more reasons to view her in a bad light. He'd already made it clear he thought she needed to improve her training skills because he constantly corrected her whenever he observed her with the dogs.

Still, she had to confide in someone. And he was here. "Weird things have been happening lately. Long before Boyd escaped prison."

His dark eyebrows drew together. "Like what?"

She took another bracing breath. Was she really going to share this with him? Did she have a choice?

"Little things," she said. "Like objects moved and doors and cabinets left open when I know they were shut." Like her clock being turned toward the wall this morning.

Had Boyd been standing at the foot of her bed? She shivered. Could there be someone else on base who had it in for her? Or was she imagining it all?

But the rose and note were real.

"Maybe whoever helped Sullivan onto base is trying to scare you," Westley said. "But why would Boyd and his accomplice want to terrorize you?"

Distaste boiled up and twisted her lips. "The only reason I can think of is because I refused a second date with Boyd during BMT."

Westley sucked in a noisy breath. "Just like a couple of the victims in Dill."

"Yes." She hated that she'd even gone on the one date, but she'd been lonely and he'd been interested. "He'd seemed charming and nice at first."

Her words gave her pause. Didn't they say that about most serial killers? Neighbors and colleagues were often shocked to learn they'd been living or working closely with someone capable of such horrendous acts.

"Then he'd made it abundantly clear he wasn't a believer. A must for me."

Was Westley a believer, she wondered. In the six months she'd been in his command, she'd never had a deep or personal conversation with him. He was too guarded, too critical. She wondered what made him tick beyond his perfectionism.

"Did he hurt you?"

The anger lacing Westley's words sent a funny little ribbon of warmth winding through her. But, of course, Westley would feel anger. In spite of his questioning if she belonged in the unit, he was a man of integrity and honor.

"No. I fended him off when he got handsy at the end of the night."

"You can take care of yourself," he said, with a good dose of pride lacing his voice, which confused her.

His words might have been a compliment, but she crossed her arms in front of her, squeezing her rib cage as tight as she could to keep from splitting into a million pieces. "There are times when I wished I didn't have to." She hated that her voice broke.

Westley dropped the lead he held and stepped on it to keep Tiger from running off, then he slipped his arms around her and drew her to his chest. He felt solid and strong. The spicy scent of his aftershave teased her senses, making the shock of his actions even more startling.

"I won't let anything happen to you," he vowed.

She believed him. Despite how infuriating she found him at times, she respected his work ethic and his diligence in making sure the dogs were well trained before being assigned a handler. He never said something he didn't mean. And he always followed through on his word.

But the last thing she needed was Westley thinking she was needy. Besides, the United States Air Force had strict rules about fraternization. She wouldn't risk her career for a hug of comfort.

She disengaged from him and stepped back seconds before a black SUV roared down the street and stopped at the curb, followed by a Security Forces vehicle.

Westley picked up Tiger's lead and had the dog heel at his side as they waited.

Tech Sergeant Linc Colson climbed out of the vehicle with his canine, a female Rottweiler named Star, but the pair hung back as Special Agent Ian Steffen from the Office of Special Investigations stepped out of the black SUV. Felicity knew the fortyish officer through her father, who'd also been a special agent with the OSI.

Ian's speculative gaze bounced between Westley and Felicity. Felicity's stomach clenched. Had Ian witnessed the hug?

"Master Sergeant James," Ian said, acknowledging Westley's salute.

Felicity raised her hand to touch her temple in respect of the man's rank.

"At ease. Are you okay, Staff Sergeant Monroe?" Ian asked.

"I am, sir." She gestured to the mailbox. "But there's that."

Ian slipped on a pair of latex gloves and removed the rose from the mailbox, placing it inside an evidence bag. He then unfolded the note and read it aloud. "'I'm coming for you.'"

The ominous words reverberated through Felicity, burning an acidic trail along her veins. There was no doubt who wrote the note. Boyd Sullivan. The Red Rose Killer.

"The crime-scene unit will dust the mailbox for prints," Ian told her as he placed the note in a separate evidence bag. "But doubtful Sullivan was dumb enough to leave any behind."

Boyd may have been a hothead and full of himself, but he'd been smart. The first time he'd gone on a rampage he'd evaded capture longer than anyone thought he would. A tremor of anxiety worked its way over her skin.

Once Ian had the rose and note stowed away, he said to her, "How are you holding up? Your father was a good man and my friend."

Tears burned her eyes. She blinked them back, along with the sharp pang of grief. "I'm managing."

He nodded, compassion softening the lines in his face. "This doesn't help. You are to come to base command with me."

"But the dogs?" Her priority—her job—was finding the canines and returning them to their kennels safely.

"I'm sure Master Sergeant James and Tech Sergeant Colson can handle the dogs," Ian stated firmly. "Lieutenant General Hall wants anyone with a connection to Boyd brought to base command."

She glanced at Westley. He gave her a slight nod.

Linc stepped up. "Actually, sir, Lieutenant General Hall would like Master Sergeant James to return to base command, as well. But we'll take the dog to the center first."

Felicity climbed in the passenger side of Ian's SUV as Westley and Tiger followed Linc and Star to the other vehicle. They drove away while Ian and Felicity waited until the crime-scene-unit techs arrived and took possession of the rose and note.

As Ian drove them to the northwest end of base, he asked, "Do you know what your father was working on prior to his death?"

Startled by the question, she shook her head. "He never divulged his cases to me."

Ian remained silent for a moment. "Do you believe his death was an accident?"

She stared at his profile. "He fell off a ladder cleaning the gutters of the house."

Yet even as the words left her mouth, the nagging thought she'd had since the moment she'd seen her father lying on the ground roared to the surface.

Graham Monroe had been an extremely cautious man. He would never have gone on the sloped roof without either someone holding the ladder, or without hooking a safety harness to the metal rung he'd attached to the roof. So why hadn't he tied off to protect himself from falling that fateful day?

Dread filled her. "Are you telling me my father's death wasn't an accident?"

Had her father been murdered?

TWO

"Dude, what were you thinking?"

Linc's pointed question stabbed at Westley. They were friends so Westley didn't take exception to the tone or the probing. Taking Felicity into his arms was a huge slip in judgment. He knew the rules. Fraternization with a subordinate could get him and her bounced out of the air force.

A stupid move.

But in that moment, she'd looked so vulnerable he couldn't stop himself from comforting her. The fact that she'd felt so right snuggled against his chest burned a hole through his heart.

She fit him…they fit together—just as he'd imagined.

For the past six months, ever since she'd walked into the training center as a newly promoted staff sergeant, her blue-green eyes sparkling and her infectious grin shining like a ray of sunshine on a cloudy day, he'd been struggling with his attraction for the rookie K-9 trainer.

It had to stop.

Hadn't he been telling himself that every day he

worked with Felicity? Yes. And every night when she would slip into his dreams.

He didn't understand it.

Not liking her should have been easy.

She was so annoyingly optimistic and bubbly. Her rookie mistakes sent his blood pressure skyrocketing and her ability to calm the dogs, though surprising and admirable, grated. Which made no sense at all.

The dogs trusted her from the get-go. And that fact told him about the type of person she was. The dogs sensed her kindness, trustworthiness and gentleness. But letting himself show any emotion regarding the rookie trainer was out of the question.

He'd even been harder on her than anyone else so no one would think he liked her. But that had only upset her, and in return made him angry at himself. He couldn't win.

All those things made his lapse in judgment minutes ago that much worse. And he had no reasonable explanation for taking her into his arms.

He had no room in his life for her. Period. He wasn't interested in forming any type of emotional bonds. He learned not to growing up, because ties only break and when they do they hurt.

He cast his eyes down, not knowing how to answer. Before he could, the tech sergeant spoke again. "Leaving the debriefing without permission wasn't cool, man," he said.

Oh. That. Yeah, the base commander, Lieutenant General Hall, and Captain Justin Blackwood, Westley's supervisor, would no doubt chew him up and spit him out with a reprimand. Westley sent Linc a sidelong glance. Did that mean Linc hadn't witnessed the embrace between Westley and Felicity?

He blew out a breath of relief.

If Felicity hadn't stepped back when she had, they'd both be in deep hot water.

"I wasn't thinking," he admitted to his friend. He ran a hand through his hair. "When I heard Felicity's name called off that list of Boyd Sullivan's potential targets, all I could think of was getting to her."

He couldn't let another person he was responsible for be hurt. Not after losing two last night.

"Excuse me?" Linc shook his head. "I don't think I want to have heard you right."

"She was supposed to be on duty last night, but she and Tamara swapped shifts."

Linc's eyes widened with understanding. "I see. Make sure you tell Lieutenant General Hall."

Westley barked out a humorless laugh. "Yeah. I will."

And he'd also have to find a way to protect Felicity and, in doing so, keep them both out of trouble.

As Ian brought the SUV to a halt in a parking spot in front of the base-command offices, Felicity stared at him. Her heart pounded in her chest as the implications bounced around her mind. "You didn't answer my question. Do you think my father's death wasn't an accident?"

"There's no evidence to suggest foul play. But the timing seemed odd," Ian admitted as he turned to face her. His eyes were troubled. "Your dad was working on a case that was highly sensitive, but we can't find his case notes or his laptop."

Anxiety slammed against her ribs. "His office was

packed up and brought to the house, but I didn't see any files or his computer."

She thought back to the box that had held pictures of her, chronicling her life from a young, gap-toothed kid to her official BMT graduation photo in her dress blues. There were the many photographs she'd taken over the years with her beloved professional-grade camera and gifted to her father to decorate his office. And, of course, all of his framed awards and certificates, a custom-made penholder and other paraphernalia that wasn't worth much beyond sentimentality.

"What about his home office?" Ian asked.

She shrugged but couldn't shake the dread crawling up her spine. "I can look. But Dad was as well-ordered and uncluttered as they come. I sorted through his desk and file cabinet searching for his will, which was filed under *W*. I didn't see any folders or files that looked official or had anything to do with his work."

She'd also found her parents' divorce papers, which had added to her sadness in the days following her father's death. Calling her mother in San Francisco with the news had been hard. Hearing her mother, usually so in control, sobbing on the other line had pierced Felicity's heart.

Her parents had still loved each other even though they'd chosen to go their separate ways. Neither had remarried. As a teen, she'd secretly hoped they'd reunite, but that had never happened.

"Are you investigating my dad's death?" she asked.

For a moment, Ian was silent, but her heart beat so loud in her ears, she was sure he heard it as well.

"Not officially," he finally replied in a measured tone. "I am looking into your father's last case. But

I'm having to start over. Now with the Red Rose Killer on base, everything else will have to be pushed to the back burner."

Her chest tightened with a wave of grief. "What was my father working on?"

Ian hesitated. "A hit-and-run off base. A witness reported seeing a Canyon Air Force Base decal on a motorcycle. Your father was trying to identify the bike and its owner."

"That's not much to go on," she said. "Many airman and officers ride motorbikes."

"True. But the last message I had from your father suggested he had a lead."

"And that person might have killed him and made it look like an accident." Sourness roiled in her stomach.

"Possibly. But keep this under wraps, okay?"

"Of course."

Digesting what Ian had told her, Felicity slowly climbed out of the SUV. Her mind spun with possibilities. Was her father's death not what it seemed?

She tripped slightly over her own feet. Everything she'd heard, everything that had happened today, was all so overwhelming.

"Steady there." She recognized the deep voice, and felt a firm hand gripping her arm.

Surprised, Felicity looked up to find Westley waiting on the walkway with Linc, Star at his heels.

Westley's touch was gentle but she shrugged off his hand, hating that he'd glimpsed her clumsiness. "I'm good."

"We dropped Tiger off at the training center," Westley told her as he fell into step with her. Linc, Star and Ian walked behind them.

They headed inside the base-command building. The four-story structure housed the administration staff as well as the photo lab and the OSI offices. Stepping into the elevator, Felicity felt dwarfed by the three men.

Even the dog made her feel tiny.

Ian, on her right, was several inches taller than her five-foot-six-inch frame, while Westley stood at least six feet tall. Behind her, Linc towered above her and Star's breath created a hot spot on the back of her leg.

Silly. She hadn't suddenly shrunk, but she stood straighter, as if an extra inch would matter. But once again, her world had been shaken and being average height wasn't enough. She wanted to be taller and stronger to better protect herself, her coworkers and the dogs.

The elevator doors swooshed open. All three men and the dog waited for her to exit before falling into step behind her. It was like leading a procession of three giant trees as they approached the base commander's office.

His assistant met them in the reception area and led them to a conference room.

"Staff Sergeant Monroe," Brenda said with a soft smile directed at Felicity, "I'm glad to see you safe and sound."

Felicity kept her expression neutral, but inside she cringed. She was trained by the best in the air force, but so were Tamara, Landon and Chief Master Sergeant Lockwood, who'd all died last night. "Thank you, ma'am," she replied politely.

"Lieutenant General Hall will see you now." She opened the door to the conference room and announced them.

"Come in." Lieutenant General Hall rose from where

he sat at the end of the long oval conference table. Tall and imposing, with his back ramrod-straight, the base commander was a force to be reckoned with. Felicity's dad had thought highly of the officer. They were on the same bowling team. Lieutenant General Hall had given the eulogy at her father's funeral. The reminder had her swallowing several times to ease the ominous tightening in her throat.

After Lieutenant General Hall returned their salute, he said, "At ease."

Felicity dropped her salute and took a position with her hands tucked at her back. Her gaze landed on another man, who had risen from his seat at the table. He was dressed in a grey business suit, but something about him led her to believe this wasn't a man to trifle with. His green eyes regarded her with curiosity and speculation.

Lieutenant General Hall resumed sitting, as did the stranger. The lieutenant general's intense grey eyes landed on Westley for a moment then moved to Felicity. "Do you know why I asked to see you?"

Refocusing on Lieutenant General Hall, she said, "Sir, I assume because of the Red Rose Killer."

"Yes. It seems Boyd Sullivan is back." There was no mistaking the hard edge of anger in his tone. "He's killed three people so far."

Another wave of grief hit her. "Yes, sir. I'd heard that."

She needed to see Maisy and offer her what comfort she could. Though having just lost her own father, Felicity knew there wasn't much comfort to be had. Losing a parent was devastating.

Lieutenant General Hall tented his fingers. "We just

received word that more people have received a rose and note like the one found in your mailbox."

Felicity sucked in a sharp breath. "Who, sir?"

"We'll get to that," he said. "First, I'd like to introduce you to Special Agent Oliver Davison of the FBI."

Oliver rose and nodded. "Since this is a federal case, I will be working with OSI and base security."

Ian stepped forward and shook Oliver's hand. "Glad to have the backup."

Felicity exchanged a confused glance with Westley. Why were she and her boss included in this meeting?

A knock sounded. Brenda opened the conference-room door. "Captain Blackwood and Lieutenant Webb have arrived, sir."

The two men, along with their canine partners, walked in. Brenda retreated and closed the door behind her.

The dogs sat at attention while the men saluted.

Lieutenant General Hall returned the salute and instructed them to relax.

As the only female soldier in a room full of handsome and higher-ranking men, Felicity's shoulder muscles tensed. But she would not allow herself to be intimidated. This wasn't the first time she'd been surrounded by men, nor would it be the last.

It's a man's world. You'll never fit in. Her mother's words when she'd learned that Felicity had enlisted echoed through her mind, but Felicity refused to accept her mother's pronouncement. Sure, Felicity had experienced some sexism over her four years of service, but it only made her more determined to prove herself worthy.

Westley stepped closer to her side. The overwhelming sense of camaraderie his nearness generated surprised her. He may be miserly with his praise and exacting in his teaching style, but her boss had her back. Which was confusing, distracting and, she had to admit, comforting.

"All of you take a seat," Lieutenant General Hall instructed.

When Westley moved to pull out a chair for her, she gave him a pointed look. He retreated but nonetheless sat in the chair beside her. The last thing she needed was him showing her deferential treatment because she was in danger.

Or was it because she was a woman? Did he see her that way?

She narrowed her eyes at him. No, that couldn't be. He was too hard on her at work for her gender to be an issue.

He raised a questioning eyebrow.

She refused to be coddled by anyone, especially Westley. She looked away.

The other men took seats, with the dogs settling behind their chairs. Ian remained standing.

"We're waiting for a few more people," General Hall said. "Would anyone like some water? Coffee?"

Everyone declined the offer.

A few moments later, Brenda escorted in three women.

When Maisy Lockwood walked in, Felicity's heart jumped. The preschool teacher's pretty eyes were red-rimmed and her countenance, usually so cheerful, was somber. Felicity gripped her chair's arms and fought for the self-control not to rush to her friend's side.

Behind Maisy came First Lieutenant Vanessa Gomez in her green nursing scrubs. Her dark hair was caught up in a clip at the back of her head and her brown eyes glowed with worry. Last to file in was Airman Yvette Crenville, the base nutritionist. The willowy blonde stopped and, with one look at those gathered in the room, seemed ready to bolt. There was no mistaking the pinch of fear in her pretty face.

After the formal greetings, the three women took seats at the table.

Lieutenant General Hall's gaze filled with sympathy. "Miss Lockwood, we are all grieving over the loss of your father."

Maisy sniffed and nodded. "Thank you, sir."

Lieutenant General Hall's gaze moved to Vanessa and Yvette. "Thank you also for coming in. You both, along with Staff Sergeant Monroe, received a red rose and threatening note from Boyd Sullivan, aka the Red Rose Killer."

Stunned, Felicity turned her gaze to the other women. After Felicity's date with Boyd, he'd moved on to Yvette, who'd also been in their BMT. The pair had dated until his discharge, when she'd publicly broken up with him. But as far as Felicity knew Vanessa, a critical care nurse, had no connection to Boyd. She'd been in officer training at the time.

"Base security will be on high alert, especially at the preschool, hospital and base housing," Lieutenant General Hall said.

"You think Boyd will come after me?" Maisy's voice rose.

"Your father was my friend," Lieutenant General Hall stated, his voice tinged in sadness. "I won't take any chances with your safety."

"I don't understand, sir," Vanessa said. "Why would Boyd target me?"

"That is an excellent question, Lieutenant," Lieutenant General Hall stated. "One I will leave to Captain Blackwood and his team to uncover. Until then your safety is our priority."

"Thank you, sir," Yvette said, her voice wobbly. "This is so scary."

"Not to worry, Airman Crenville," Lieutenant General Hall replied in a soothing tone. "Boyd will be captured quickly."

Yvette shivered. "I hope so."

Sweeping his gaze over the female personnel, Lieutenant General Hall said, "The four of you are dismissed."

Felicity rose with the others but paused as Westley stood and touched her arm.

"Wait for me in the hall," he said in a low voice.

She blinked at the request. She wanted to ask him why, but her desire to talk to Maisy overrode her curiosity. She nodded and hurried after Maisy. She snagged her friend by the elbow once they were in the hall. "Oh, honey, I was so sorry to hear about your dad."

Maisy's eyes filled with tears. "It was horrible."

Felicity drew Maisy to a bench along the wall as Vanessa and Yvette walked away. "Here…sit."

Maisy sat and wiped at her eyes. "I don't understand how this could happen."

Neither could Felicity. The whole thing seemed surreal. Boyd Sullivan escaping prison, getting on base in the dark of night and killing three people and terrorizing three more. She prayed God would bring Boyd to justice quickly.

"He took my dad's cross necklace," Maisy said, drawing Felicity's attention.

That was odd. Boyd hadn't collected souvenirs from his past victims. At least not that Felicity recalled. What did it mean when a serial killer changed his MO?

She shuddered with anxiety, afraid they were going to find out before all was said and done.

When the door closed behind the women, Westley had to fight to remain in place and not follow Felicity out. He didn't like not having eyes on her. If anything happened to her…

"Have a seat," Lieutenant General Hall told the men who had stood as the ladies left the room.

The men resettled themselves in their seats around the conference table, all attention focused on the base commander.

Lieutenant General Hall pinned Westley to his chair with an intense stare. "Master Sergeant James, care to explain why you left the meeting earlier without permission?"

Westley sat up straighter, glad Felicity was in the hall and not witness to his dressing down. He gave the lieutenant general his reason, hoping he didn't reveal more than concern for his employee.

"It appears you were right to be alarmed for her welfare," Lieutenant General Hall said. "I'll overlook your lack of protocol this one time."

Easing out a relieved breath, Westley inclined his head. "Thank you, sir."

"Now, how do we ferret out the person who helped Sullivan get on base?" Lieutenant General Hall's gaze traveled over the men at the table and settled on Oliver Davison. "What can you tell us about the prison break?"

"We've confirmed Sullivan bribed two guards into letting him out of his cell and into the docking bay, where he crawled into the back of a laundry truck and escaped," Oliver said.

Westley's phone buzzed with another incoming text from the training center. He glanced at it and was glad to read the growing total of dogs recovered.

Lieutenant General Hall focused on Captain Justin Blackwood. "How did he get on base?"

"Sir, we're still working on that," Justin replied. He sat at the table with his hands braced on his knees. "All personnel are being asked to report their whereabouts for the past twenty-four hours. It will take us time to verify every alibi."

"And what of Sullivan's half-sister?" Oliver asked. He consulted his notebook. "Staff Sergeant Zoe Sullivan."

"We are looking into her, sir." Linc spoke up for the first time. He'd taken a position leaning against the wall rather than sitting at the table. "She's a flight instructor and is currently in the air. But when she lands, we'll be questioning her."

"Keep me informed of your progress," Lieutenant General Hall said. He trained his gaze on Justin. "You also received a rose and note, did you not?"

Justin nodded. "Yes, sir."

Surprise washed through Westley.

Oliver asked Justin, "What has Sullivan got against you?"

"I was one of his basic instructors, sir," Justin replied. "I called him on the carpet on multiple occasions for slacking off and harassing the female recruits."

"Stay vigilant, Captain," Lieutenant General Hall instructed.

"I will, sir."

To Westley, Lieutenant General Hall said, "How are you progressing on recovering the dogs?"

"We have half recovered so far, sir." Not nearly enough. There were still so many dogs missing. Westley hated to think about what could happen to the dogs if they made their way off base or deep into the woods or onto the runway. "Everyone on base is helping to bring the dogs in safely."

"Excellent." Lieutenant General Hall turned to First Lieutenant Ethan Webb. "What I'm about to tell you doesn't leave this room."

"Yes, sir," Westley murmured in agreement along with the others.

"It seems Sullivan has been busy," Lieutenant General Hall said. "Either before coming here or shortly after, he visited Baylor marine base and left a rose and note for Lieutenant Jillian Masters."

Westley's gaze shot to Ethan, who sat across the table. Jillian was Ethan's ex-wife, though she'd retaken her maiden name. "Why would she be a target?"

Ethan's jaw firmed. "Jillian had a run-in with Boyd shortly before his discharge. She'd been on base observing a K-9 seminar I was conducting. This was back when we were married. Boyd tried flirting with her, and it didn't go over well. Jillian can be…cutting when she wants."

Westley had only met the woman once. She'd definitely had an edge to her.

"But we don't know when Sullivan was at Baylor?" Linc said. "He may not be on base now."

"We can't assume anything," the OSI agent, Ian Steffen, stated. "We have five known targets. We need to be vigilant and catch him, if and when, he makes a move."

Acid churned in Westley's gut at the thought of Felicity in danger. Granted, she was in the law-enforcement track and trained to take care of herself, but so were Sullivan's other victims, and yet the fiend had killed three well-trained airmen.

At least with her at the training center, he'd be able to keep an eye on her during the day. He'd ask for permission to send home a German shepherd named Glory to protect her at night. Glory was a fierce dog with great protective instincts.

Hall slammed a palm on the table. "I will not have this maniac running rampant on my base."

"If I may suggest," Ian said, "you reassign Staff Sergeant Monroe to a more visible base position, where she will draw Boyd out in the open. Sullivan has to know security will be beefed up at the training center now, especially with two homicides on site."

Westley's heart pounded as the agent's words echoed through the room. "You want to make her a sacrificial lamb?" The thought of deliberately putting her in harm's way made his blood run cold.

"You don't think she's up to the task?" Ian asked, his tone soft but intense.

Westley didn't doubt Felicity's abilities. He just didn't like tempting danger. Not when that danger was in the form of Boyd Sullivan, a man who had already killed eight people. "No. I mean, she'll be safer at the training center."

Ian arched an eyebrow. "Duly noted. However, of the three female targets, she's the only one in the law-enforcement track."

Lieutenant General Hall sat back and rubbed his chin. "The base photographer is being transferred to another assignment. Does Staff Sergeant Monroe know her way around a camera?"

"I can answer that, sir," Ian said. "I know for a fact that she does. Her father's office was covered with photos she'd taken."

Westley had seen her with a nice camera on numerous occasions, taking pictures of the dogs. And he'd seen the images. Though she'd claimed photography was a hobby, as far as he was concerned, her work was professional-grade.

But Westley couldn't protect Felicity if she wasn't at the training center. Responsibility weighed heavy on his shoulders. Knowing he was going out on a very thin and fragile limb, Westley met the OSI agent's gaze. "I want to be detailed to her protection."

Ian studied him with speculation in his eyes. "I see no issue with that."

Surprised at the lack of argument from the agent, Westley went even farther out on the limb and addressed the lieutenant general. "And I want a dog to be with her at all times. Even at night." Asking for something that traditionally wasn't allowed was risky. Every military working dog was a valuable asset and when not deployed was kept in the kennels at the training center.

Lieutenant General Hall studied him for a moment. "Okay. I will allow it. Use the dogs as needed during this situation." He sat back. "Then it's settled. Staff Sergeant Monroe will be transferred to the photo lab under my command." Lieutenant General Hall zeroed his gaze on Westley. "And you will be detailed to her protection along with a canine." Lieutenant General Hall turned to Justin. "You good?"

Justin nodded. "Yes, sir."

Westley sucked in a quick breath of triumph and nervousness. That meant he was going to be Felicity's shadow 24/7. Keeping an emotional distance when they'd be so close would be harder.

But if he failed to protect her, she could be the next victim. He couldn't allow that to happen. Wouldn't allow it to happen. If anything happened to Felicity, he'd crumble beneath the weight of guilt.

He'd walk on coals if need be. Anything to protect her.

"She will be your responsibility to keep safe, Master Sergeant James." Lieutenant General Hall's gaze narrowed. "Are you up to the task?"

Pulse spiking, Westley nodded. "Yes, sir."

Game on.

THREE

The door to the conference room opened, drawing Felicity's attention away from Maisy. Westley stepped into the hall and beckoned Felicity back inside.

"Just a second," she called to him. Turning to Maisy, she said, "Did you drive over?"

Maisy nodded. "Yes." She rose and hitched her purse higher on her shoulder. "I have to get to church to teach my Sunday school class."

"Are you sure you're up for that?"

"Yes. I need to be with the kids." Maisy hugged Felicity. "Be careful."

"You, too." Felicity stepped back. "I'll call you later."

Maisy smiled and hurried out of base command.

Squaring her shoulders, Felicity met Westley at the door. The hard light in his eyes didn't bode well and a hundred thoughts—none of them good—raced through her mind.

"Is everything okay?" she whispered.

He didn't reply. Instead he stepped aside so she could reenter the conference room. She held her salute until the base commander told her to relax.

Lieutenant General Hall regarded her steadily. "I understand you know how to work a camera."

Surprise washed through her. "Yes, sir."

"Excellent. You are being reassigned to the photo lab effective immediately."

"Excuse me?" Felicity stared at the lieutenant general then her gaze darted to Westley. His inscrutable expression irked her. Had he signed off on this transfer? She didn't want to leave the training center. She wanted to work with the dogs. Was this photo-lab assignment some sort of punishment? Had Westley used the situation as an opportunity to have her removed from the training center?

Lieutenant General Hall held up a hand. "Now, hear us out." He nodded at the OSI agent.

Ian tipped his chin at her. "Of the potential victims, you're the only one trained to handle the likes of Boyd Sullivan."

His words sounded like a compliment. Still, confusion pounded at her temples. She glanced around the room at the men seated at the conference room table. When Westley had requested she rejoin them a few minutes ago, she'd had no idea what to expect. Certainly not this. "What do you want from me?"

"You take on the role of base photographer," Ian said. "This allows you to be visible, to roam the base at will taking many, many photos."

"You'll then upload the images to our database," the FBI agent said. "We'll run the pictures through our facial-recognition software. If Boyd is on base and you can capture his image then we'll have a better chance of finding him before he hurts anyone else."

She turned this over in her head. Her gaze strayed

to Westley again. The muscle in his jaw ticked, as if he was clenching his teeth. Was he upset or happy to be rid of her? She didn't know. He was so hard to read.

Her gaze swept over the other men staring at her and waiting for a response. How did one reply to being asked to act as bait for a serial killer?

But Ian was correct. No way could Yvette or Vanessa take on the role, despite the training all air-force personnel went through. Felicity imagined her father would want her to take on the challenge. Her mother, on the other hand, would flip out when she learned about this. Not that Felicity had any intention of telling her mother until after the fact. Or ever.

Straightening her shoulders and standing tall, she turned her attention to Lieutenant General Hall. "I will do whatever is needed, sir."

Approval shone in his eyes. "Well done. Then I will let you and Agent Steffen work out the details. You'll report for duty in the photo lab tomorrow morning."

"Yes, sir."

Lieutenant General Hall looked to Ian. "I'll let you take it from here."

"Take a seat," Ian told her as he pinned her with his gaze. "I'm not going to lie to you. This could be dangerous. We don't know what Boyd will do. We do know he is ruthless and cunning."

Swallowing back the trepidation clawing up her throat, she nodded. "I understand, sir."

"Despite his objections to your new assignment, Master Sergeant James has volunteered to be detailed to your protection."

Felicity absorbed the information like a blow to the gut. Why had Westley objected? She didn't want to jump to conclusions, but she was…disappointed. "I don't need Master Sergeant James's protection."

Ian raised his eyebrows. "It's not up for debate, Staff Sergeant Monroe."

She slanted a glance at Westley. He stared at her with a hooded gaze that made her fingers curl in her lap. "Who will run the training center?"

"I'll check in often with the center, but Master Sergeant Streeter will take over until Boyd is caught and put back in prison," Westley stated in a tight voice.

Caleb Streeter was a seasoned trainer and more than capable of handling the center. But he wasn't a master level trainer like Westley. She didn't understand how he could give up control. He ran the center like his own personal company. His way or the highway.

She wanted to ask Westley why he'd volunteered and why he disapproved of her taking the photography position, but with so many people staring at her, she decided her questions would have to wait.

She returned her attention back to Ian, who regarded her closely. No doubt he was waiting to see if she was going to continue to argue. No way. She wouldn't be that person. She was up for taking down the Red Rose Killer. She nodded her head in acquiescence.

"Now that that's settled," Ian said. "We are forming a task force to include all of you. We will add to it, as we need. But for now, all information is to be kept confidential. We don't want the base or the general public to be aware of what we are doing to bring Boyd to justice. A traitor on this base is helping Boyd. We don't know who it is." He turned his gaze to Justin. "We need to find this traitor, Captain."

"We're doing our best, sir," Justin said. "We will interview everyone on base."

"Who were Boyd's friends on base?" Oliver asked.

Felicity noticed the look exchanged between Justin and Linc before Justin spoke again. "Boyd was buddies with Airman Jim Ahern, who works in aircraft maintenance."

"We will be questioning him," Linc said.

"Good," Oliver said. "I want to be there when you do."

"Yes, sir," Linc and Justin both said.

"I want you all to report back here tomorrow at sixteen hundred with updates." Lieutenant General Hall rose. Everyone in the room snapped to attention.

"You all have your orders," Lieutenant General Hall said. "I have arrangements to make with Miss Lockwood for her father's service." He walked out.

As Felicity and Westley headed for the door, Ian said, "Staff Sergeant Monroe, if you'd wait a moment. I'd like to speak to you privately."

The scowl spreading over Westley's features made Felicity tense.

Finally, he directed his gaze on her. "I'll wait in the hall."

She nodded and sat down.

Westley walked out, followed by the others. When she and Ian were alone, Ian said, "I want you to search your house for anything that might be related to your father's last case. Tell no one. We don't know who to trust."

She swallowed the burn of wariness. "Yes, sir."

Whoever had been in her house might also be looking for her father's case notes. A shiver ran over her.

And that would mean her father hadn't died by an accidental fall…

She fought to catch her breath.

He *had* been murdered.

Numbed by the realization, she left the conference room.

True to his word, she found Westley waiting for her in the hallway. She wanted to tell him about her conversation with the OSI agent, about the case her father was working on and the fact that maybe she wasn't going crazy. But Ian's words reverberated through her head.

We don't know who to trust.

"What did Agent Steffen want?"

From the paleness of Felicity's face, Westley guessed something significant. And the way she stared at him, with wariness in her blue-green eyes, sent a fissure of alarm sliding down his spine.

She shook her head. "Nothing that I want to talk about."

So there was something, but she didn't trust him enough to share. Hurt spread through his chest. How could he protect her if she distrusted him? And why did she distrust him? Hadn't he always treated her professionally? Except when he'd hugged her in a moment of weakness. That was something he wouldn't let happen again.

Did she know about his mom and dad? Is that what the OSI agent told her?

Swallowing his concern, he led her toward the exit.

A bulldog of a man rushed through the double doors of the base command. He wore the airman battle-ready uniform with a staff-sergeant insignia and the name

Dooley on the tag. The solid occupational badge marked him an engineer.

Westley swiftly maneuvered Felicity behind him. For all Westley knew, Boyd could be posing as an airman and using disguises to camouflage his appearance.

"Felicity!" the man exclaimed and hurried toward them. As he drew closer, Westley realized the man was older than he first appeared. Mid- to late-fifties.

Felicity nudged Westley aside. "Uncle Patrick."

Westley relaxed and stepped back, allowing Felicity room.

Patrick skidded to a halt and eyed Westley, saluted and then turned his gaze on Felicity. "Are you okay? I heard the Red Rose Killer is loose on base and that you were threatened."

"I'm fine, Uncle," she replied. "A little shaken, that's all."

"I would imagine so," Patrick said. "Colleen must be beside herself."

Felicity made a face. "I haven't told Mom and would rather you didn't as well."

Patrick smirked. "The last thing I want is to be the bearer of bad news to my sister." He gave a mock shudder.

"Uncle, this is Master Sergeant Westley James," Felicity said. "Westley, my uncle, Staff Sergeant Patrick Dooley."

"You're from the MWD training center, right?" Patrick asked. "I've seen you working the dogs."

"That's right." From Patrick's tone, Westley gathered the man wasn't a fan of the canines.

Patrick focused on Felicity. "It's not safe for you to

go home. You need to come stay with me. We're family after all."

The stiffness in Felicity's shoulders told Westley she wasn't keen on the idea. "She'll have all the protection she needs," Westley assured the man. "We're heading to the training center now to pick up a dog for her."

Felicity shot Westley a look that he couldn't decipher. He guessed she was thinking that it was against regulations for an MWD to be housed anywhere but in the kennels. He would have to explain when her uncle wasn't present.

Patrick's upper lip curled slightly. "Unacceptable. Your mother would never forgive me if I let something happen to you when I could keep you safe."

"I appreciate the offer, Uncle Patrick," she said. "But Westley will provide me the protection I need."

"I suppose you'll be safe at the training center as well." Patrick didn't sound mollified.

"Actually, I'm taking over the role of base photographer starting tomorrow," Felicity told him.

The man's eyes nearly bugged out of his head. "What? Whose crazy idea was that? You'll be out in the open. Exposed. Unacceptable!"

Though Westley agreed with the man's assertions, he remained silent. He would let Felicity fill in her uncle on Westley's role.

"The base commander's order," she said. "And Master Sergeant James will be with me."

Westley met Patrick's narrowed gaze. "You'd better keep her safe."

"I plan to," he replied.

Felicity let out a small huff of air. "We need to get back to the training center so I can collect my things."

Patrick walked outside with them. The temperature had risen on this April afternoon, warming the air to a nice muggy level that immediately dampened Westley's skin. Walking to the other side of base wasn't an appealing thought. "Patrick, would you give us a ride back to the training center?"

"Of course," he said and led them to a jeep parked across the road.

The vehicle smelled faintly of a scent Westley couldn't identify. He rolled down the window for fresh air. The ride to the center took all of four minutes.

Felicity gave her uncle a quick hug before he drove away, leaving them standing outside of the center.

"I didn't realize you had more family on base," Westley said as they walked toward the entrance.

"We aren't super close," she confessed. "Uncle Patrick and my dad used to be friends when they were young. That's how my parents met, but as Dad moved up through the ranks and into the OSI, he and Patrick grew apart." She let out a bitter-sounding laugh. "My parents grew apart, as well."

"Divorced?"

"Yes." She stopped to glance his way and shielded her eyes from the sun. "What about your parents?"

Acid churned in his gut. He had to ask, had to know. "What did Agent Steffen tell you?"

"Why do you assume he told me anything about you?"

"Because something he said upset you," Westley replied. "Something that you don't trust me enough to talk about, so I gathered that meant he warned you off of me."

Speculation entered her blue-green gaze. "No. What we talked about had nothing to do with you."

Relief swept through him. And he felt idiotic for his paranoia. "Good." He started walking again, intending to put the whole subject behind them.

She hurried to keep up the pace and put a hand on his arm before he could open the door to the training center. "But now I'm curious. You never talk about yourself. Why would I need to be warned off of you?"

Westley's mouth turned to cotton. Of course. The woman was curious. Felicity liked to talk and to hear others' stories. He'd seen and heard her on numerous occasions with the handlers that came to the training center and with the other trainers. She had a way about her that people found engaging and comfortable.

Right now, he felt anything but comfortable. He wasn't going to spill his guts about his past if he didn't have to. The things his parents had done didn't have anything to do with his present life. Nor with his ability to protect Felicity. "Sorry. Not going there."

"I know you're my superior, and I'm to follow orders," she replied, "but I figure since we're going to be stuck together for the foreseeable future, we may as well get to know each other a bit better."

He faced her. "There's nothing to know."

"Sure there is. Where did you grow up?"

The determination in her expression didn't bode well. The tenacity that would make her a great dog trainer one day also meant he wasn't getting out of this conversation easily. The only thing to do was give her the basics that anyone could read in his official personnel file. "I grew up in Stillwater, Oklahoma. My father passed on years ago." In prison, but he kept that tidbit to himself.

"And my mother is…" He didn't know where Lori Jean James was. Last he'd heard from her, she'd been in Nevada. "We aren't close."

"I'm sorry," Felicity said.

Her compassion annoyed him. He didn't want her pity. "Look. None of that matters. I have one focus right now. That is protecting you." He yanked open the door. "The first thing we need to do is find Glory. She'll be the best dog for you."

He didn't need to read Felicity's mind to know she wasn't pleased with him. It was written in the tiny *V* between her eyebrows and the irritation in her eyes.

Inside the center, Felicity went to gather her things from the locker room, while Westley headed for the dog kennels at the back of the building. He passed one of the long-time trainers, Rusty Morton. Westley liked the guy well enough.

Rusty paused to salute. "Master Sergeant."

Westley returned the customary salute. "At ease. How is it going?"

Rusty relaxed. "I'm headed out to see if I can find more of the dogs. Someone reported seeing some in the woods at the far edge of base."

That was concerning. Six hundred acres of rough terrain and steep canyons could pose a danger to the canines. He hoped nothing bad befell the dogs. "I'll be praying you find them." And praying the canines were unharmed. "I'll head out soon to search as well."

"Yes, sir." Rusty hurried away.

Why Westley clung to the faith of his childhood, he didn't know. Habit maybe. Or deep inside, maybe he still wanted to believe God answered prayers. So he prayed that Rusty and the other trainers out searching for the dogs had success.

Westley entered the large open space where numerous kennels lined the walls. Dogs barked in greeting. He was pleased to see so many of the dogs had been returned unharmed.

"We have about sixty dogs still missing," Caleb Streeter told him. The tall, muscular officer was refilling water bowls. Because Caleb and Westley were the same rank, they dispensed with the protocol of saluting.

Westley was surprised by the number and tried not to be disheartened. The dogs had to be somewhere on base. But where?

"I need Glory," Westley said as he stopped in front of her empty crate. "Where is she?"

"She's one of the sixty."

"No way!" Westley couldn't believe it. "Glory is a rock star. She'd come when called."

"I know. I don't get it," Caleb said. "Liberty, Patriot and Scout are missing, too."

"That's just weird." And worrisome. Westley rubbed the back of his neck, where tension had taken up residence. The four German shepherds were superstars in the making and very valuable to the military. They should have been easily recalled. He hoped and prayed they weren't hurt, or worse. Anxiety ate at his gut.

His gaze collided with the dark eyes of an all-black German shepherd named Dakota. A measure of relief eased some of the pressure knotting his muscles. Dakota was a good candidate for Felicity. The mature, multipurpose dog excelled in his training and had a good balance of aggression and excitability that was needed for patrol work. He'd been deployed with his handler on two missions overseas before coming back to the training center to be paired with a new handler after his handler had been injured. "You'll do nicely, Dakota."

The dog perked up hearing his name. Grabbing a lead, Westley released the dog from his kennel and latched the lead to his black collar. The dog was a two-year-old veteran well trained in protection. Westley was confident that Dakota would keep Felicity safe.

Westley explained to Caleb the situation of the Red Rose Killer and Westley's detail to Felicity's protection.

"Man, that's rough," the other trainer said. "What can I do to help?"

"I need you to take over the day-to-day tasks while I'm on this detail."

Caleb's blue eyes grew wide. "You got it."

Surprisingly, Westley didn't mind giving up control of the program. It was only temporary and he knew the dogs would be in capable hands. Taking Dakota with him, he went to find Felicity, who was talking with base reporter Lieutenant Heidi Jenks in the training center break room.

He saluted the officer while Dakota sat at attention.

"At ease," Heidi said as she returned the salute.

Turning his gaze on Felicity, he hoped she hadn't given away any details. "What's going on?"

Felicity smiled easily. "Just chatting. Do you know Heidi? She's my neighbor."

"Only by reputation," he replied.

Pushing back her long blond hair, Heidi said, "I was hoping you all could tell me about the missing dogs and the two trainers who were murdered here last night."

"No comment," Westley replied. "Felicity, we need to go."

Heidi scrambled from her chair. "Wait. Give me something. Do you have any info on Chief Master Sergeant Lockwood's murder?"

"Sorry, Lieutenant. You'll have to contact the base commander for information." He gripped Felicity by the elbow and hurried her out of the center. Once they were away from the reporter, he said, "What did you tell her?"

"Nothing," she replied. "I know better than that. My dad was OSI, you know."

"Right." He took his cell phone from his pocket and sent a text to the training staff telling them Caleb would be in charge and not to talk to the press.

"I thought you said Glory was the dog for me," Felicity said, petting Dakota. "Not that I'm complaining. I like this guy a lot."

Westley relayed what Caleb had told him as they hurried toward base housing.

"I have to believe we'll find the dogs," she said, though a thread of anxiety wove through her tone.

"Ever the optimist, aren't you?" he replied.

"Is that a bad thing?"

He shrugged. "It leaves you open to disappointment."

"Maybe. But if I go around expecting disappointment then I'm sure to find it."

He marveled at the way her brain worked.

"Would you mind if we say a prayer for the dogs' safety?" she asked, her eyes searching his face.

"Be my guest," he said. He'd like to think God would hear and deliver on their request. Maybe he would for Felicity.

She bowed her head. "Lord God, please watch over the missing dogs and bring them back safely. Watch over the whole base, Lord. Keep everyone safe from Boyd Sullivan. Amen."

"Amen," he mumbled.

When they reached her house, crime-scene tape fluttered around the mailbox, slamming home the reminder of the danger lurking on base.

Before Felicity could step inside, Westley halted her with a hand on her shoulder. "Let Dakota go first." If the Red Rose Killer was waiting inside, the dog would alert.

He unhooked the lead from the dog's collar. "Search," Westley told Dakota.

The dog went inside. Westley tensed, waiting for some sign of alert to trouble. A few moments later, Dakota returned without alerting.

"It's safe," Westley said.

Felicity stepped inside and let out an audible gasp.

Westley followed her, taking in the disarray of the living room. Either she was a messy housekeeper or someone had ransacked her house.

FOUR

Felicity clenched her fists at her sides, taking in the damage done to her house while she'd been at the briefing.

The stuffing from the couches littered the floor like little puffy clouds. All the books from the shelves were strewn about. Framed photos had been knocked off the walls, the glass shattered. A sense of violation seeped through her bones.

The blatant destruction was worse than the subtle signs of intrusion that had caused her to question her sanity. Now she knew without a doubt she wasn't going crazy. Someone had been in her house, searched her house. Was it the person who killed her father?

Dread nipped at her. Had the person found what they were looking for? Was it the evidence in her father's last case that had gone missing?

If so, then what chance did the OSI have of catching the person who took her father from her?

"I take it this isn't how you left things this morning." He took out his phone and reported the break-in to base security.

Westley's wry comment grated on her already taut nerves.

She whirled on him. "No. This is the work of a killer."

"Why would Boyd want to wreck your house?"

She snapped her jaw closed and clenched her teeth. Should she confide in Westley? The question poked at her like a cattle prod. Ian had said not to trust anyone.

Agitated, she hurried through the house, seeing the same sort of ransacking in every room, though her bedroom wasn't nearly as torn apart. But the majority of the chaos was concentrated in her father's office. His file cabinets had been emptied, his desk drawers dumped in heaps.

"Someone seemed to be searching for something important to them," Westley mused.

She wondered how much help he could be in figuring out the mystery. The man was smart.

Aware of Westley and Dakota dogging her steps, she wrestled with the need to tell Westley the truth. There was no reason why she shouldn't trust this man. Working for him for six months had shown her he was a man of integrity. Surely, he wasn't involved in her father's death. Yet, reluctance kept her silent.

He cocked his head and studied her. Dakota sat and mimicked the man. Felicity shook her head, amused despite the circumstances. Seemed like both males were analyzing her.

"What aren't you telling me?"

Westley's question jerked her gaze to meet his intense stare. Her heart pounded as her instinct warred with Ian's directive.

"Felicity, I can't protect you if I don't know what is going on."

True. Westley was the only one standing between her and a potential killer.

Two killers, in fact.

And if Westley didn't know there was more than one threat out there, then how effective could he be? And once Westley knew everything, he could help catch her father's murderer. She'd ask Ian for forgiveness later.

"This wasn't the work of Boyd Sullivan. At least, I don't believe so." There was the slimmest possibilities Boyd or his accomplice had trashed her home, though their motive was a mystery.

Westley's eyebrows rose. "Then who? Why?"

She inhaled, blew out the breath and then said, "My father's death wasn't an accident."

Westley frowned. "What do you mean? How so?"

Her stomach clenched. "Agent Steffen believes that the last case my dad was working on is why he's dead. My father had a lead on a hit-and-run off base. His case notes are missing."

"So that's what Agent Steffen wanted to talk to you about. He thinks your father's death was no accident. That he was…murdered?"

Bile rose to burn her throat. "Yes."

"Felicity—"

She could hear the need to comfort her that had been in his voice earlier, when he hugged her. "Don't. Please, Westley, just don't. Not now."

Westley rubbed a hand over his jaw. "Okay. Okay." He looked around the office. "So this was someone looking for the evidence your father had."

Grateful he was refocusing on something they could both handle, Felicity blew out another agitated breath.

"I believe so. The question is did they find what they were looking for?"

"This morning, when you thought there was someone in your house, there really was."

The grim reality of how vulnerable she'd been sent a shiver of terror down her spine. To cover her fright, she bent to pick up a broken picture frame.

"Don't." He echoed her plea; only from him, the word was a command.

She stilled.

"The Security Forces crime-scene techs need to dust for prints and look for particulates."

Of course. She straightened and stared down at the smiling face of her father, his arm wrapped around her on her sixteenth birthday. Tears burned her eyes. She held them back. No way would she cry in front of Westley. "I miss him so much."

"He was proud of you," Westley said.

She lifted her gaze to him in surprise. "That's kind of you to say."

"It's the truth. He came to the training center not long before his death and watched you putting Riff through his paces," Westley told her.

That's right. She'd been so nervous knowing her father was there. She'd tried extra hard to do everything perfectly. And Riff, thankfully, had cooperated on that day. She hoped someone found him soon and returned him to the training center.

"He asked me how you were doing. If I thought you were in the right place."

Her stomach sank. She braced herself. "And what did you tell him?"

"That you have the makings of a good trainer," Westley replied.

She swallowed the lump of emotion clogging her throat. "You did?"

"Yes. I could tell he was pleased."

Love for her father swelled in her chest. "Do you believe that I'll make a good trainer?"

"I do. In time."

She held his gaze as his words slid into her, bolstering her confidence. That was the closest Westley had come to giving her a compliment on her work. Being the youngest and newest trainer, she tried so hard to earn his approval. Instead, most of the time she earned only a scowl from the handsome, buttoned-down master sergeant.

He cleared his throat and averted his gaze but not before she saw a softening in his eyes that sent a flutter through her. He wasn't scowling at her now.

She swallowed and tried to make sense of the change in her boss. Well, he was no longer her CO. Now he was her protector.

Gesturing to the front door, he said, "Let's wait outside."

With Dakota at their heels, they walked out to the porch.

Felicity leaned against the railing and faced him. The need to make sure they were on equal footing forced words from her mouth. "I'm trusting you to keep me safe. I'm trusting you with the knowledge that my dad's death was more than it seems."

Westley braced his feet apart and returned her gaze. "I'm honored. On both accounts."

She narrowed her eyes. She toggled two fingers between them. "But this has to be a two-way street. You must trust me, as well. I'm not some wilting lily for you to prop up."

A small smile curved his lips. "Duly noted."

Annoyance buzzed around her head like a million tiny mosquitoes. It was like doing her absolute best to prove herself yet again and falling short.

A flush of frustration heated her skin. "I need to know that you won't keep secrets from me. If something comes up with Boyd or the investigation into my father's death, you can't try to protect me by not telling me."

All humor left his face. His jaw firmed. "If you need to know I'll tell you."

"No. That's exactly what I mean." She pushed off the railing. "If we're to do this, we're all in together. You don't get to decide what's right for me. Not you, or anyone."

"Aren't you tired of carrying that chip on your shoulder all the time?" he commented softly.

Her eyebrows shot up. "What do you mean? I'm just trying to do my best."

"But you don't have to do this alone," he countered.

"As my supervisor, I took instructions from you. But now, you're not my boss. I want to make sure we are clear on that."

"Crystal."

He stepped closer, forcing her to tilt her head to look up at him. She found herself fascinated with the little gold specks surrounding his dark irises, making the outer rim of blue even brighter up close. There was so much in his gaze that confused and confounded her. Determination. A spark of anger. And something else that had her pulse leaping.

What was going on? This was her superior. The man who never stopped watching her so he could find a fault.

"But make no mistake, Felicity." His deep voice commanded her attention. "My mission is to protect you. Whatever it takes. If I tell you to duck, you'd better duck. I refuse to have your stubbornness cost you your life."

Felicity swallowed hard. She hated the way his words wound through her, conjuring up horrifying images of death and destruction. "I am not stubborn."

His mouth softened and his eyes sparkled. "Your stubbornness is one of your most appealing traits."

He found her appealing? Whoa. That was unexpected.

She blew out a breath, unsure what to say or how to feel. The line between them that always seemed so clear at the training center was now blurring.

Before she could reply, several vehicles roared to a stop in front of her little house. Best to let his comment go. She didn't want to care what Westley thought of her.

But what she wanted and what happened were rarely the same thing.

Westley watched the play of sparks in Felicity's eyes and pressed his lips together to keep from grinning. He'd surprised her with his comment. Good. He wanted to keep her on her toes. She needed to stay sharp if they were going up against two deadly threats.

Turning his attention away from the lovely staff sergeant, Westley greeted Captain Justin Blackwood and the OSI agent, Ian Steffen, with a salute. Two base-security policemen followed with crime-scene kits in hand.

"What happened?" Justin asked. "Did Boyd Sullivan break in?"

Westley exchanged a quick glance with Felicity. A red rose and ominous note this morning and now an intruder in her house. It made sense the captain would ask about Boyd.

"We don't know, sir," Westley said. "Someone broke in and ransacked the place. It's obvious they were looking for something."

Justin pinned Felicity with a questioning look. "Any ideas what they were searching for?"

Felicity's gaze darted to Ian. Westley figured she was looking to the agent for permission to speak about their suspicions regarding her father's death.

Ian gave a subtle nod before stepping forward. "I can answer that, but first, please direct your men to process the scene. This is for your ears only."

Justin's gaze narrowed, but he motioned for the two MPs to proceed into the house. When the two men were out of earshot, Justin said, "Explain."

"Prior to OSI Agent Monroe's death, he was working on several cases that are still open," Ian said.

Justin swept a hand toward the house. "Then this isn't related to the Red Rose Killer?"

Ian shrugged. "Hard to say. From what I've read on Boyd Sullivan, this isn't part of his MO."

"Neither is taking jewelry from his victims," Felicity interjected.

All eyes turned to her.

"Maisy told me that her father's cross, the one he always wore, was missing when she found him."

Westley heard the subtle pain in her tone. She hurt for her friend. He told himself the sharp constriction in his chest was for *both* women's losses.

"Captain Blackwood," Ian said, "I suggest conferring with the sheriff's deputy in Dill, Texas. The one who brought down Sullivan the first time around. She may have some insight into his psyche that might help us find him."

"Good idea," Justin said. His next comment was cut off when his cell phone rang. "Excuse me." He stepped away to take the call.

"Better to keep the focus on Sullivan," Ian said in a quiet tone.

Westley could only guess the OSI agent didn't want to advertise the fact that Felicity's father had been murdered.

If the killer thought he had gotten away with the break-in attributed to the Red Rose Killer, the more likely he, or she, would make a mistake. Westley sent up a silent prayer that God would let justice be done on earth for her father.

When Justin returned, his blue eyes were troubled. "We've got a missing cook. Airman Stephen Butler didn't show up to his shift in the commissary today. But his car was found in the driveway of his base housing."

"Are you thinking he's another of Boyd's victims?" Westley asked.

"We'll see. I'm headed over to inspect the car." To Westley, Justin said, "Keep in touch with me." His gaze slid to Felicity as he turned. "We'll see you both tomorrow morning back at base command."

Once Justin's vehicle disappeared from sight, Ian ushered them inside.

Westley kept Dakota at his side as the two crime-scene techs were packing up their equipment.

"Did you find anything worth noting?" Ian asked them.

"No, sir," the older of the two said. "We've collected

prints and will run them through the databases and compare them to Agent Monroe and his daughter." He nodded at Felicity in deference.

She smiled back at him. "Thank you."

If they found prints that didn't belong to her or her father, then they could have a lead on the intruder. Westley hoped it would be that easy.

Once the two techs had left, the trio gathered in her father's office. Westley released Dakota. The dog sniffed at the floor and moved around, inspecting the room. A large mahogany L-shaped desk took up half the space and a large black captain's chair sat behind the desk. Filing cabinets and a bookshelf filled in the remaining space and more of Felicity's photos decorated the wall.

The pictures were good. Ian had been right. She knew what she was doing with a camera.

"Felicity has explained to you my suspicions about Graham's death?" Ian asked Westley as he hitched a hip on the edge of the desk.

"She has, sir." Worry camped in his gut. "Why hasn't there been an official investigation?"

Ian's expression turned even more grim. "There's no evidence to follow. Only my gut feeling that the case Graham was working on had turned deadly. I've tried to piece together what I can from the civilian police report."

"Which is?" Westley asked.

"In a rather suspect neighborhood of San Antonio, a motorcycle struck a civilian and left the scene. The bike had a Canyon Air Force Base sticker on the back. The witness could only say the rider was dressed all in black to match his bike."

"The victim?" Felicity asked.

"Broken back. Paralyzed from the waist down."

Empathy dampened her eyes. "That's horrible."

Westley hated the thought that someone from the base would be so dishonorable as to leave the scene. Unless the hit wasn't an accident. A foul taste rose from his stomach. "Was the victim targeted?"

"Not that I can tell," Ian said. "It seems more like a bad case of 'wrong place, wrong time' on both sides. The roads were slick from a recent rain. The streetlights were out when the pedestrian stepped off the curb into the path of the bike."

"Do we know what Agent Monroe's case files look like?" Westley asked as he picked up a stack of file folders. "Were they in a notebook or in a folder like these?"

"Dad kept meticulous records," Felicity said. "But I don't know how he managed his work cases." She looked to Ian. "Have you found my dad's laptop?"

Ian shook his head.

Felicity frowned. "I haven't seen his laptop here. I've been through his safe and nothing important was in there."

"We need to find that computer," Ian stated. "His notes and the lead he was working on will be on the hard drive."

Westley's blood pressure rose. "We're going to have to work on the assumption that this guy didn't find the computer based on the condition of the house. We need to keep her safe."

"Which is why you're here, Master Sergeant James."

Westley pulled in a bracing breath and met Felicity's gaze. She rolled her eyes in response. Oh, yeah. This was going to be fun.

Ian headed toward the door. "I need to focus on the hunt for Boyd Sullivan. I trust you two will be circumspect in searching for Graham's case notes and his computer. I hate to think someone in the OSI could be involved, but as far as I know Graham didn't share with anyone that he had a lead that would break the hit-and-run case."

"Yes, sir," Westley assured him. "We'll keep our investigation on the down low."

"You'll let us know if you hear any more about what Boyd is up to?" Felicity asked. "I'm praying he left the base now that everyone is looking for him."

"One can hope so," Ian said as he left the house.

When they were alone, Westley asked, "Where else could your father have hidden his laptop?"

Felicity thought for a moment. Her gaze lifted to the ceiling. "There's an attic crawl space used for storage."

"Let's go check it out," Westley said. "Dakota," he called to the black German shepherd who had taken an interest in her father's desk.

Dakota had dropped to his belly and crawled beneath the desk until only his tail poked out. When the dog tried to back out, the whole desk shook. Dakota growled, his paws digging into the carpet as he tugged.

Westley hurried over, kneeled and peered under the desk. Needing light, he took his Maglite from his utility belt and aimed it into the space. Felicity scooted in on her knees and pressed close to Westley. He had to fight to keep focused on the dog rather than on the soft curves melding into him and the vanilla scent of her hair teasing his senses.

Dakota's collar had caught on a metal latch in the side of the wood desk.

Felicity dropped onto her belly and wiggled her way farther beneath the desk.

"There's a secret compartment. Dakota must have followed my dad's scent under here," she said with excitement ringing in her voice. "But I can't release the latch or unhook his collar."

"Let me." Westley squeezed in next to her. "Hold this."

He handed off the flashlight. Her slim fingers closed over his, creating warm spots on his skin before she relieved him of the device. He flexed his hand and then grasped the little metal hook. The awkward position didn't make it easy, but he managed to unlatch the door which popped open, freeing Dakota. The dog quickly scrambled away from the desk.

Felicity shone the beam of light into the compartment.

"What's that?" Felicity reached past him to grasped what was in the secret cubby. They both shimmied out from beneath the desk.

Felicity held up her find.

A key with strange grooves along the blade and an oblong bow with a cutout in the center glinted in the light.

He met her confused gaze. "Any idea what the key opens?"

She shook her head. "I don't. But the key has to be important if Dad hid it."

Westley had to agree. Whatever the key opened would lead them to her father's killer. He knew it in his bones. But how would they find the lock?

FIVE

Shaken to her core at finding the key hidden in her father's desk, Felicity's fingers trembled. In them she held the one clue that could lead them to her father's murderer.

Westley helped Felicity to her feet. His big, strong, capable hands dwarfed hers, making her feel feminine and treasured. For a moment, she wanted to hang on to him in case she needed steadying. If she was honest with herself she'd admit she liked having him close after such a horrible day. He was solid and secure. And she found herself wanting to lean on him for support.

But she squared her shoulders, took a breath and stepped away from him, forcing him to release her. She had to stay strong. Not show any weakness.

He tucked his hands into the pockets of his uniform jacket.

Holding up the key to inspect it, she said, "I've never seen this before."

"Could it be to his desk at the OSI office?" Westley asked.

"Ian said Dad's desk had been emptied."

"Maybe a footlocker or gym locker?"

"Dad used the base rec-center gym, but the lockers there have combination locks on them." She walked to the office closet and opened the door. "Dad's old service footlocker is in here." She pushed back a rack of coats. "It doesn't have a lock on it, though."

"Maybe the key goes to something inside the locker?" Westley suggested.

"Maybe." She tugged the box from the closet. Westley hurried over to help her. His nearness did funny things to her insides. She should have felt crowded, but instead she was comforted by his presence. Maybe that was why she'd felt the urge to hang on to him when she stood. She was glad she wasn't going through this alone.

She lifted the lid and surveyed the contents. A folded flag, boxes holding her father's service medals and a stack of letters in her mother's handwriting bound by a rubber band.

Westley rocked back on his heels. "Would your father have stashed his laptop in here?"

"Doubtful," she said as she closed the lid with disappointment. "And if he had, the computer's gone now."

"We need to take the key to Ian," Westley said. "Do you want me to hold it for safekeeping?"

"We do need to take the key to him. But until then I'll keep it." Her father had hidden the key for a reason. Until she knew the reason, the key stayed with a Monroe.

She reached beneath the collar of her uniform and tugged out a gold chain with a delicate cross that her grandmother had given to her on her sixteenth birthday. She quickly undid the clasp and slipped the key onto the chain before rehooking the clasp. She let the necklace rest against her uniform.

Placing a hand over it and taking solace from the tiny reminder of Grandma Esther, she said, "Where I go, it goes."

A low growl emanated from Dakota seconds before they heard heavy footsteps in the living room.

With a hand on his sidearm, Westley positioned himself in front of Felicity. Dakota stepped in front of Westley, his tail up, his ears back. Tension radiated from the dog.

Felicity froze, once again wishing she had her own sidearm. She'd talk to Lieutenant General Hall about it tomorrow. For now, she stayed rooted to the spot behind her two protective males.

"Felicity!"

Recognizing her uncle's voice, Westley relaxed and gave Dakota the hand signal to stand down.

Pushing past Westley, Felicity called out, "Coming." She quickly tucked the necklace back beneath her uniform before hurrying out of the office. She didn't need to tell Westley not to mention the key. No reason to get her uncle needlessly worked up about her father's death when they had no hard evidence to prove he'd been murdered.

Westley and Dakota followed right behind her. They found Patrick standing in the middle of the living room with his mouth agape. He rushed to Felicity and pulled her into a crushing hug. "Are you okay? I heard something happened here. Who did this? Did the Red Rose Killer come back?"

"I don't know, Uncle," she said, her voice muffled in his shoulder. He smelled of the cigars he relished and Old Spice. His uniform was rough against her cheek.

"See, I told you, you need to come stay with me until

this madman is captured," Patrick said. He pulled back to stare at her with worry lines crinkling his forehead. "If anything happened to you—" He blew out a noisy breath. "My sister couldn't take the shock."

Felicity appreciated his concern but she didn't want to dwell on her mother's reaction. "Nothing is going to happen to me. As you can see, I've got protection. Dakota and Westley will keep me safe."

Patrick's lip curled as he eyed the dog.

"He's a good dog. Protective." Felicity knew from her mother that Uncle Patrick had had a bad childhood experience with a dog.

Patrick met her gaze. Concern darkened his expression. "You shouldn't stay here, though," he argued. "Look at this place. It's a mess."

"It's my home," she said. "I'll clean it up. I'm not letting the likes of Boyd Sullivan drive me out of the house I shared with Dad."

Patrick dropped his chin slightly. "Your father is gone, pumpkin. He wouldn't want you to risk your life by staying here out of sentimentality."

"It's not sentimentality," she replied. "It would be too hard to pack up and move. Besides, if Boyd is on base and watching, then he'd know where I was going."

Patrick frowned. "I don't like it."

"Neither do I," Westley said.

Felicity's gaze whipped to him. Figures he'd side with her uncle.

Westley held up a hand as if to ward off an argument from her. "But Felicity is correct. Any move would draw more attention to her. Dakota will be staying with her, and I'll be close by at all times."

She smiled reassuringly at Patrick. "See. I'll be taken

care of." It grated to say that. She could take care of herself. But then again…if she'd truly been Boyd's intended target last night at the kennels, she clearly needed the backup.

"If you're sure." Patrick rubbed the back of his neck. "I could stay here with you."

"No!" She practically shouted the word and then grimaced at the sound of panic in her voice. The last thing she wanted was to have her uncle fussing over her. He'd be pushy like her mother. "I mean…no, thank you. I don't want to put you out. I'll be fine."

Patrick glanced around and then his gaze settled back on her. "You have my number. If you need me for anything, you ring me. I'll check in with you often."

Deciding that was as good as she'd get, she nodded. "That would be great. I'll call if I need to."

"All right, then." Patrick narrowed his gaze on Westley. He spared Dakota a parting glance and a shudder, then said, "Promise me you won't let anything happen to her."

"I promise."

Westley's deep voice wrapped around her. He was a man who kept his promises, but how could he make this one when there was no guarantee he could keep it?

Felicity eyed the Office of Special Investigations. They were here to bring the key to Agent Steffen, though she wasn't sure that it mattered. She doubted Ian would know what the key unlocked.

They'd driven over in her two-door compact car with Dakota sitting on the back seat. Westley hadn't balked when Felicity had climbed into the driver's seat. She'd been half-convinced she'd have to argue with him to drive her own car, but instead he'd relaxed into the passenger seat after adjusting it to accommodate his long legs. His wide shoulders took up the whole seat and hovered close to her shoulder. If she leaned a little to the right, they'd be touching, which made her hyperaware of every bump in the road.

She'd parked in front of the building and now she hesitated. She hadn't been to her father's office since his death. Memories threatened to swamp her. She fought them back with as much energy as she could spare, afraid if she didn't keep them at bay she'd drown.

She forced herself to slip out of the car and meet Westley and Dakota on the sidewalk. She noticed that Westley's gaze scanned the area, his hands on his utility belt, before he gave her a nod to indicate she should go ahead of him.

The receptionist smiled softly at her with sadness filling her eyes. Felicity had known her since she was ten. The tears were hot on the back of her throat. She could feel Westley's gaze, but she didn't dare look at him or the tears would start flowing. She had to be strong. They had a killer to catch. And a mystery to solve.

She led the way down the hall. The building was quiet on this late Sunday afternoon. The carpet beneath their feet snagged at Dakota's nails.

Felicity stopped short outside a closed door halfway down the hall. Her father's name still graced the name plaque. A spasm of longing hit her. On a whim, she slipped the key from beneath her uniform jacket and took off the necklace.

"Worth a try," she murmured at Westley's questioning look. She put the key in the lock. It didn't fit. She hadn't really expected it to. If the key was so important that her father went to the trouble of hiding it in a secret compartment in his desk, it wouldn't be so mundane as to be a key to his office.

"Is the door locked?" Westley asked.

She tried the handle. It opened easily. She stepped inside and breathed in. She knew it was a trick of her mind, but she inhaled the lingering scent of her dad's citrus aftershave. Her heart ached and grief twisted in her belly.

The office walls had been stripped of the framed photos and certificates that had once decorated the space. The desk was bare and the filing cabinet drawers were open and empty. She wasn't sure why seeing the space so barren left her feeling empty and grief-stricken.

She guessed the reality that he was truly gone couldn't be denied here. At home, his things were still touchable, as if waiting for his return. Maybe her uncle was right. Maybe she was staying in the house out of sentiment.

Her friend Rae Fallon, a rookie fighter pilot, needed a roommate. Maybe Felicity should consider moving into Rae's apartment.

She shrugged off her thoughts. Right now, she and Westley had a task to do. She couldn't let herself fall down a rabbit hole of sorrow.

Turning to leave, she bumped into Westley. His hands steadied her. She couldn't deny she liked the way warmth seeped through her jacket to touch her skin. She looked into his eyes. The compassion in his gaze brought on a burn of tears. She blinked to keep them at bay.

"It's okay to grieve," he said. "You've been so strong this past month."

"I grieve," she said. "In private." Where no one could judge her for the noisy sobs and the red-rimmed eyes.

"I want you to know you don't have to keep everything in all the time," he said.

She shrugged away his hands. "You sound like a shrink."

His mouth lifted at one corner. "Doling out advice I was given a long time ago."

She recalled he'd mentioned his father had passed on. "How old were you when your father died?"

Westley stepped back, his expression closing like a door in her face. "Seventeen."

"Had he been ill?" she asked gently.

"Let's just say things weren't good and leave it at that." He gestured toward the door. "We need to see Ian."

Obviously, Westley had no intention of sharing his past with her. To him, she was an assignment. Nothing more. She couldn't help disappointment from burrowing deep inside, even though she knew it was silly of her to feel anything where Westley was concerned. Better for them both to remain detached.

Westley moved to the exit with Dakota at his side. He stopped in the doorway, looking both ways before allowing her to exit in front of him.

They knocked on Ian's office door. It whipped open and Ian's eyebrows rose in surprise. "Is something wrong?"

"We think we found something important," Felicity said and showed him the key while explaining about the secret compartment in her father's home desk.

He waved them inside the office and examined the key. "You have no idea what the key opens?"

"None," she and Westley said in unison. They stood shoulder-to-shoulder facing the older man.

"Neither do I." Ian handed the key back to Felicity. "It could be nothing."

She frowned. "But why would he hide this then?"

"I don't think that's relevant to your father's murder. For all we know the key could have been in the desk for years. The piece was an antique when he bought it, right?"

Her shoulders slumped. She hadn't thought of that. Maybe the key wasn't her father's. Her fingers closed around the piece of metal, the edges digging into her skin. She'd really hoped she'd found the means to uncover her father's murderer.

Ian picked up his jacket and shrugged it on. "Right now, I have to focus on the Red Rose Killer."

Her stomach knotted. "Has Boyd Sullivan struck again?"

By the grim set of Ian's jaw she knew the answer before he spoke. "We believe so. The commissary cook that had been reported missing this morning, Stephen Butler, is dead. His body was found in a trash bin of an off-base local restaurant. His uniform and ID weren't found at the scene."

"Boyd dressed like Stephen and used his credentials to get on base," Westley stated.

"That's the going theory," Ian replied. "I'm heading to the morgue to verify the cause and time of death." He met Felicity's gaze. "Be careful. I'll see you both tomorrow morning."

Felicity and Westley walked out with Ian. As they

entered the reception area a man rushed forward, holding a cell phone. Felicity winced at the sight of base reporter John Robinson. With his red hair and horn-rimmed glasses, he looked more like a caricature than a serious journalist.

"Agent Steffen," John said, holding out the phone with the speaker pointed at Ian. "What can you tell me about the Red Rose Killer? Have there been any more developments?"

"No comment," Ian said with a frown and continued walking.

John shoved the phone in Felicity's face. "You're a target. Why would Boyd Sullivan, known as the Red Rose Killer, want to hurt you?"

Following Ian's lead, Felicity said, "No comment." She and Westley pushed past the reporter.

"Aww, come on, guys," John complained as he followed them out to the sidewalk. "The base is in an uproar. The personnel deserve to know what's going on."

Westley put up a hand to prevent John from following them. "Lieutenant General Hall will make a statement when he is ready. Until then, back off."

John's mouth turned into a petulant scowl. "What is the lead MWD trainer and—" John flicked a glance at Dakota "—a guard dog doing in the OSI offices? Are you providing protection for Staff Sergeant Monroe?"

Westley stepped into John's space and stared him down. Dakota growled, clearly sensing his handler's tension. "I said back off."

John held up his hands and moved away. "Fine."

Felicity glanced at Westley, glad she wasn't the one at the wrong end of his anger. When he put his hand to the small of her back to propel her down the sidewalk, heat seared through her uniform to warm her skin.

"You handled him well," she commented.

Westley blew out a breath. "He's harmless, but I don't want him making a pest of himself to you. The last thing we need is a nosey reporter poking around into what we're doing. If we're going to find the lock that key belongs to, we need to fly under the radar with our investigation."

She paused to stare at him. "So you believe the key is important?"

He seemed to contemplate the question. "My gut tells me yes. But maybe it's wishful thinking."

That she understood. "I feel the same. The key looks old, but not like an antique."

"It won't hurt anything for us to keep our eyes open for a lock that it might fit," he said.

"Sounds good to me." She was glad to know he was on the same page as far as finding her father's killer. "The goal is to attract Boyd but not the attention of anyone else."

"Right." Westley's phone dinged. He checked the incoming text message. "A couple more dogs have been found."

"That's good." She sent up a prayer that all the animals would be recovered safely. "What is the total count now?"

"We're still missing over forty dogs," he replied. "I can't grasp that Glory, Patriot, Liberty and Scout haven't returned."

"That's strange," she said. Worry twisted through her. "You don't think anything bad happened to them, do you?"

"I hope not. The dogs are valuable. All of them," he said. "But those four are our cream of the crop."

In his tone she heard the same anxiety she felt. Before she thought better of it, she threaded her fingers through his and gave his hand a squeeze. "They will be found."

"I wish I had your confidence," he said as he paused to open the driver's side of her car. "I hope they didn't find a way off the base."

"That would be scary," she said.

A Security Forces vehicle rolled up behind them and Ethan Webb leaned an elbow on the open windowsill. "Hey, you two. Where are you headed?"

Felicity assumed they'd go back to her house, but then her stomach rumbled, making her aware she hadn't eaten more than a few bites of the lunch she'd grabbed at the training center before she and Westley had gone to her house. She wondered if Westley had eaten today.

"I'm starving," she announced rather unceremoniously.

Both men stared at her.

She shrugged. There wasn't much in the way of groceries at home. "I want tacos and chips and salsa from La Taqueria."

Westley chuckled, a sound that sent a little tingle down her spine. "Then the BX it is."

The BX was the base's shopping center filled with popular restaurants and dry-good stores.

"I'll join you after I kennel, my partner, Titus," Ethan said.

"We need to take Dakota to the training center as well, so he can have his dinner," Westley said.

"Meet you there." Ethan drove away.

Felicity drove to the training center. Once there, they fed Dakota and checked on the dogs. Then they met Ethan outside. He was talking to Rusty.

Westley returned the salute. "Caleb tells me you brought in Winnie and Lacy."

Rusty nodded. His hazel eyes were troubled. "Yes, sir. They were wandering around the church grounds. Pastor Harmon called."

"There are more out there," Westley replied, a note of anxiety threaded through his words. "We need to find those dogs."

"Yes, sir." Rusty hustled away.

"You could have told him he'd done a good job," Felicity said to Westley. "A little encouragement goes a long way."

Westley cocked his head and studied her. "You don't think I'm encouraging?"

She barely stifled a snort. "No. You tend to be direct with your criticism and withhold your praise. And frankly—" She lifted her chin. Time to stand up to him and say what she'd been holding in for months. "It bugs me. It would be nice if every once in a while you said 'Well done. Good job. Way to go. You did good.'"

Westley raised an eyebrow. "If I'm not correcting you, you're doing it right."

The urge to roll her eyes was strong but she resisted and smiled sweetly. "Sometimes it's helpful to hear some encouragement."

"I'll take that under advisement," he said in a tone that grated on her nerves.

Ethan's laugh reminded her they weren't alone. "You two sound like an old married couple."

Felicity shot Ethan a glare. "Not even."

"We're moving from hungry to *hangry*," Westley murmured.

She opened her mouth to ask him how he dared to say that, but then she realized he was correct. Her hunger was making her irritable. "You're right." She sighed. "Can we go now?"

"I'll meet you there," Ethan said and headed to his vehicle.

"Your chariot awaits," Westley said with humor in his expression as he gestured to her car. Her insides turned to liquid and her heart did a little two-step in her chest.

The old adage Be Careful What You Wish For came to mind as he grinned at her. She'd wondered what it would be like to see him really smile when the force of a small grin was like taking a set of paws in the gut. How on earth was she going to survive spending so much time with him if he could make her knees weak with one grin?

SIX

Sated, Westley pushed his empty plate away. He'd enjoyed this respite except for the weight of the missing dogs pressing on his mind. The restaurant was noisy with conversation and music playing from speakers in the corner. A television attached to the wall showed a muted soccer game. Every time one of the two teams scored, the crowd cheered. Westley and Felicity sat side by side with their backs to the wall. He liked being able to see who was coming their way and to observe the crowd.

Plus, he wouldn't deny he liked having Felicity within arm's reach. In case of a threat, he told himself. Not because she was a beautiful woman. Which wasn't the best path for his thoughts to wander down, especially after nearly telling her about his father.

That kind of slip wouldn't be productive. The last thing he wanted was her pity.

Her anger he could take. She could chew him out all she wanted about not giving praise. He'd turned out just fine without receiving any.

Ethan Webb and Linc Colson occupied the other two seats at the table. Linc had arrived a few minutes after them. Apparently, Ethan had called him on his way to the eatery.

Westley couldn't remember the last time he'd sat in a restaurant with those he considered friends. Most of his meals were frozen, microwavable dishes eaten in the training-center break room. This was a nice change. He only wished it hadn't come at the cost of so many lives.

"I heard you mention you had leave coming up," Felicity said to Ethan. "Any fun plans?"

"Nothing firm," he replied. "After being overseas, it will be good to relax."

Having never been deployed, Westley could only imagine Ethan's need for some downtime.

A tall muscular man stopped by their table.

"Hey, Isaac," Westley said, standing to shake the Senior Airman's hand. "I'd heard you were back."

Isaac Goddard was a former combat pilot recently returned from Afghanistan.

"Yes, it's good to be home." Isaac's green eyes rested a moment on Felicity. "Hello."

She smiled at him. "Hi. We haven't met." She held out a hand. "Felicity Monroe."

The two shook hands and a strange sense of possessiveness spread through Westley. He wanted to put his arm around Felicity and claim her as his. Instead, he said, "You know Ethan and Linc?"

The other men rose to shake Isaac's hand and clap him on the back.

"Welcome home," Linc said.

"I heard you're trying to bring home a dog from Afghanistan," Ethan said.

Isaac nodded, his expression haunted. "That's right. I filed the paperwork to have Beacon sent to me."

Curious, Westley asked, "Is the dog injured?"

"No, he's a hero." Isaac rubbed his chin. "He saved my life."

"What kind of dog is Beacon?" Felicity asked.

"A German shepherd. I really hope the brass will let me bring him to the States. I'm afraid of what will happen to him if he stays there."

"We'll pray you and Beacon are reunited," Felicity said in a gentle tone.

Tenderness filled Westley at her thoughtful comment.

Isaac gave her an odd look. "Okay. Anything that helps. I'll see you all around." He walked away and they took their seats.

Felicity leaned close. "Uh-oh, here comes Heidi."

Sure enough, the female base reporter weaved her way through the crowded tables, heading straight for them. "Incoming," he said to the others.

Ethan and Linc swiveled to see who was approaching. Because they were in a casual setting, they dispensed with the formal salute.

As soon as Heidi reached the table, Linc held up a hand to the base reporter. "No comment."

"I know, I know," she said and adjusted her dark-framed glasses. "You all can't talk about the Red Rose Killer. That's not why I'm here."

Westley wasn't buying it. "Then why are you here?"

Heidi pointed to Felicity. "I understand you're being reassigned to the photo lab."

"Where did you hear that?" Westley asked. It wasn't a secret, or at least it wouldn't be once Felicity started roaming the base with her camera. But it was still disconcerting to know the information was out there already.

"I never reveal my sources," she said. "Is it true?"

Felicity sighed. "Yes, it is. Lieutenant General Hall asked if I'd take on the position because the current photographer is transferring off base."

Heidi edged closer to the table and took a notebook and pen from her purse. "Felicity, is this reassignment really because you're a target of Boyd Sullivan?"

"Hey," Ethan objected. "Didn't we just establish we're not discussing him?"

Heidi's eyebrows drew together, but she didn't acknowledge Ethan's words. "What qualifications do you have to be base photographer? Formal training?"

"I've taken some photography classes," Felicity replied.

Heidi made a note. "Won any awards? Had your work displayed in a gallery?"

Felicity shook her head and a red flush crept into her cheeks. "No."

Sensing how uncomfortable Felicity was, Westley said, "Enough with the questions. Lieutenant General Hall feels she's a good fit for the job. That's all that matters."

Heidi hitched the strap of her purse higher on her shoulder over her standard blue short-sleeve service shirt. "And I'm trying to do my job."

Felicity put a hand on his arm. "It's all right." To Heidi she said, "I'll be photographing the BMT graduates and their families Thursday. You might want to come and see how it goes."

There was gratitude in Heidi's smile. "I will. Thank you." She glanced around the table. "Are you all going to the memorial service tonight at the Canyon Christian Church? I understand Pastor Harmon will be doing a special tribute to the victims."

Westley's gut clenched. Felicity's fingers tightened on his arm. He could feel the tremor traveling through her. He covered her hand, offering what little comfort he could.

"Yes," Felicity said. "We're going."

Ethan and Linc nodded also.

"Then I will see you there." Heidi pivoted on her black flats and wove her way out of the restaurant.

"How did she know you were here?" Ethan asked Felicity.

Felicity shrugged. "I guess the base grapevine is alive and well."

Westley signaled to the waitress they were ready for their check.

After paying their bill, Westley and Felicity left the restaurant.

"I'd like to go home and freshen up before the service tonight," Felicity said as she put her car in Reverse.

"Of course," he said. "Let's stop by the training center so I can do the same. Then we'll go to your place."

She pursed her lips. "You really aren't going to let me out of your sight, are you?"

"Not if I can help it." He was tasked with keeping her safe. More like he'd demanded the detail, but he didn't need to explain that tidbit to her.

The Canyon Christian Church pews were filled as Felicity, with Westley at her side, filed into the large sanctuary. Everyone was standing, with arms around each other, as they sang "Amazing Grace."

Memories of her father's memorial service played through Felicity's mind. She'd sat in the front row with her mother at her side. They'd held on to each other in their grief while Pastor Harmon had spoken about her father's years of service and dedication to his country and his family. Felicity's heart had broken over the senseless accident.

But it wasn't an accident. He'd been murdered.

Acid burned through her chest. She placed her hand over her heart, feeling the outline of the key beneath her dress uniform.

"This way," Westley whispered in her ear, drawing her back to the present.

He guided her to a pew on the right, where an airman shuffled over to make room for them. Westley stepped aside so she could move past him. She couldn't stop herself from giving him an appreciative glance. He wore his dress uniform well.

The navy jacket fit his broad shoulders and tapered down to his trim waist. She thought him handsome in his battle-ready uniform and in civilian clothes, but in the dress blues, he was hotter than the Texas sun in July.

She gave herself a mental head slap as she stood next to her friend Rae Fallon, a rookie fighter pilot. Rae smiled at her with sad eyes and put her arm through Felicity's.

Emotion welled within Felicity as Westley placed his arm around her waist. His compassion and willingness to comfort her in public sent surprise cascading over her, warming her from the inside out. But then the rational side of her brain kicked in. Everyone had an arm around the person next to them. He was simply following suit. She wouldn't read more in to it. Instead she focused on how good it was to be a part of something so much bigger than herself. And seeing the camaraderie among her fellow servicemen and -women gave her comfort.

When the music ended, everyone sat and Pastor Harmon approached the podium. On the big screens behind him, four images appeared—Airman Landon Martelli, Airman Tamara Peterson, Airman Stephen Bulter and basic military training commander Chief Master Sergeant Clint Lockwood.

Tears sprang to Felicity's eyes. Her heart hurt for the loss of the fellow MWD K-9 trainers, the commissary cook and the father of her friend Maisy.

After Pastor Harmon's touching eulogy for the murdered air-force personnel, Felicity and Westley left the church with the crowd.

"We'll head back to the training center to grab Dakota before going to your house," Westley told her.

She nodded. Her spirit felt heavy with the weight of grief and anger. Why had Boyd come back to the base to kill? Why hadn't he just disappeared once he escaped prison? She could only imagine how warped his mind was to make him risk returning to Canyon to spread his evil.

"Westley," Captain Justin Blackwood called from the sidewalk, where he stood with his sixteen-year-old daughter, Portia, who'd only a year ago come to live with Justin after her mother died.

Felicity and Westley veered off their path and stopped by Justin. "Sir," Westley said with a salute. Felicity followed suit.

Justin returned their greeting with his own salute. Felicity had to press her lips together to stop a smile when she noticed Portia roll her eyes and duck her head to stare at her phone.

Felicity remembered what it was like to be the daughter of an officer in the United States Air Force. All the protocols, the pomp and circumstance, that to a young girl seemed over-the-top. But Felicity had grown to appreciate the steady nature of the military. She hoped one day Portia would as well.

"How are we with the dog situation?" Justin asked.

"Rounding up more every hour, sir," Westley replied.

"Good." He rubbed a hand over his jaw. "Now if we could only find Boyd Sullivan. We found out how he got on base."

"We heard," Westley said. "But once on base, someone had to have hid him. Do we know who yet?"

"Unfortunately, no. But we're still combing through the personnel, looking for anything that might point to his accomplice."

"Did someone talk to his half sister?" Felicity asked.

"She's been questioned. She admitted to visiting her brother in prison but denies helping him in any way. Do you know her?"

"We've met briefly, but no, I don't know her," Felicity replied. Even though the base could feel small and isolated at times, there were too many people on base to become friends with everyone.

Justin nodded, his gaze going to something over her shoulder. She turned to see Heidi standing close by. Boy, she never gave up.

Felicity turned back toward the captain and noticed the other base reporter, John Robinson, lurking by the lamppost, obviously trying to eavesdrop on their conversation. They clearly had a tag team going. She nudged Westley and directed his attention to John.

Westley shook his head. "Vultures. Sir, we should table any more discussion until the meeting tomorrow."

"Agreed. Good night. Be careful," Justin said before turning away and ushering his daughter to the parking lot.

Because the church was only a few blocks from the training center, they had parked there and, walked over. Now twilight had slipped to night. A million stars twinkled in the sky and the moon rose in a crescent over the base. In some ways so ordinary. A typical night in Texas. However, today had been anything but ordinary.

Four people were dead.

A killer was on the loose.

And she'd learned her father's death had been murder.

Tension coiled through her as she walked. Her pace picked up.

"Eager to get home?" Westley murmured as he matched her stride.

"Eager to put this day behind me," she replied.

He snorted his agreement and slipped a warm hand around her elbow. It was a gentlemanly gesture. Protective. Possessive.

Her heart fluttered.

In a panic, her gaze leaped to the stop sign ahead as if her brain was sending her a warning.

Don't go any further with that train of thought.

Letting herself believe his actions had any deeper meaning beyond protecting her from Boyd Sullivan was foolish.

The crowd from the church thinned the farther away

they walked from the building. They passed the dentist offices and rec center. The veterinarian clinic's lights were on and Felicity waved to the receptionist in the window. As they crossed the parking lot for the vet clinic, the sound of an engine turning over marred the quiet night. Odd. The streetlamp that normally kept the lot lit up at night was dark.

"Hurry," Westley said.

Sensing his tension, she quickened her pace even more. Tires squealed as a car shot forward. Felicity caught a glimpse of a chrome grill before Westley's arm snaked around her waist and he lifted her off the ground.

With her wrapped in his arms, he dove out of the way seconds before the vehicle roared past, barely missing them. They landed hard on the pavement, Westley taking the brunt of the fall, Felicity landing on top of him. For a long, silent moment neither moved.

Heart in her throat, she said, "Are you okay?"

He grunted in reply. "Up."

Realizing she was squishing his midsection, she disentangled herself from his hold and rolled to the side in a sitting position. In the dark, she reached for him, finding his shoulder as he sat up.

"That was close."

She sucked in a breath at his words. Too close. Someone had tried to run them down. "That was a base vehicle. One they use to move the planes."

"We need to alert security."

"Can you stand?" she asked.

"Yes," he barked out.

She didn't take his tone personally as she rose and helped him to his feet. He was allowed to be cranky after dodging a speeding truck. "Thank you for saving my life."

"Saved both our bacon," he said. "That maniac would have mowed us both over."

"True," she said past the tension lodged in her chest like a rock.

Only when they were inside the training center did she see that Westley's uniform jacket was ripped at the elbow and blood seeped from a scrape. While he made the call to Security Forces, she went in search of gauze and alcohol wipes.

She ran in to Bobby Stevens, an airman and new trainer who'd only been at the center for a month.

"Hey, Bobby," she said.

He saluted. His gaze took in the items she held. "Everything okay?"

"Westley's injured," she told him. "I got it."

"What happened?" Bobby followed her to Westley's office, where he was still on the phone.

Not sure she if should say anything, remembering Ian's warning of not trusting anyone, she fudged. "A little mishap, that's all."

Westley ended his call and said, "Bobby. How are the dogs?"

"Good, sir," Bobby replied with a salute.

Westley returned the salute with a wince. No doubt from his injured elbow. "Make sure to let the vet know if any of the dogs seem off. You never know what any one of them could have eaten."

Bobby nodded and hurried away.

To Felicity, Westley said, "Let's get Dakota and go."

She frowned and held up the gauze and wipes. "Let me dress your wound."

"Later." He came around his desk and went to a closet, where he grabbed a duffel bag. "Let's go."

By the time they made it outside with Dakota trotting alongside them, two Security Forces vehicles rolled to a stop. Linc hopped out of one and Justin out of the other.

Justin strode to their side. "What happened?"

After Westley explained, Felicity spoke up. "I recognized the vehicle as one of the trucks that push the planes around the runway."

"Did you get the license number?" Linc asked.

"It had been removed," she told them.

To Linc, Justin said, "Put out an alert. Anyone sees one of those trucks missing a plate needs to report in." Linc nodded and headed back to his vehicle. To Westley and Felicity Justin asked, "Any chance you saw the driver?"

They both shook their heads.

"We were too busy diving out of the way," Westley remarked drily.

Justin rubbed his chin. "Last we heard, a civilian reported spotting Boyd a few hours away. But that person could be mistaken and he could actually be on base."

"Or the driver could be someone else," Felicity said. Her gaze met Westley's.

"The one who ransacked your house?" Justin looked thoughtful. "Why try to hurt you?"

She didn't have an answer. It was one thing to think the villain was searching for the file on the hit-and-run. Now was he trying to kill her?

A shiver of fear went through her. Dakota edged closer and touched his nose to her hand. The dog apparently sensed her upset.

"I'm taking Felicity home," Westley said. "Dakota and I will be on twenty-four-hour duty."

Felicity wanted to say that it wasn't necessary, but she wasn't about to put herself in a vulnerable position just because she was uncomfortable with the idea of Westley in her home.

Though *uncomfortable* wasn't exactly the right word. More like she'd be hyperaware of him and that would mess with her head. She was struggling as it was to keep her feelings from veering into territory she'd rather not explore. Yet, she couldn't come up with a logical protest that wouldn't reveal her feelings.

"All right then. Stay safe." Justin drove away, as did Linc.

Deciding it would be better to take the small SUV Westley used for transporting dogs across base, they left her car parked in the lot. They loaded Dakota into the back and then both climbed in the front. After buckling up, she turned to Westley. His strong jaw was set in a tense line. His capable hands gripped the steering wheel.

Emotion clogged her throat. He'd risked his life for her. And she had no doubt he would do so again if necessary.

"Thank you again. I appreciate your willingness to see to my safety." Inwardly she groaned at the stiff and formal way she spoke when she was nervous.

Westley sat silent for a moment, then he looked at her. "The truth is I should have known that car was there. I should have been prepared for something to happen. I won't be caught unaware again."

"Please, you couldn't have foreseen the near miss with the base truck. I didn't see it."

"But it's my job to see the threat before it gets to you."

"You're not a superhero," she said.

He snorted. "Maybe that's what you need. Someone else who will protect you better."

A flutter of panic hit her out of the blue. "Stop it. I want you to protect me. Now start this car and get us home." She sat back and tried not to think about how true those words were. She couldn't imagine putting her life into anyone else's hands.

But what about her heart? Was that safe as well?

I want you to protect me.

As Westley sat on the leather couch in the living room of the Monroe home, Felicity's words reverberated through his mind.

She had no idea how much those words rocked his world. No one had ever wanted him for anything. Not his father or his mother. Not the foster parents he'd been sloughed off to after his mom had dumped him off at child protective services. Okay, that wasn't totally accurate. There had been one foster mother who had treated him with kindness, but then he'd been yanked from the home after a fight with another foster kid.

He'd hardened his heart long ago against the need to be wanted.

But with those words Felicity had turned him to mush.

As he helped her put her house back in order, he'd tried to keep an emotional and physical distance. He'd been relieved when she'd finally bid him good-night and had gone upstairs.

Above his head a floorboard creaked. He was hypersensitive to every movement she made as she settled in for the night.

He leaned back against the cushion. From this vantage point he had a clear view of the front door, the back door and the door to the garage. Dakota laid down across the threshold to the stairs after he'd done a perimeter check. They were on guard and ready, should any danger appear.

Felicity was as safe as they could make her.

Even still, Westley sent up a prayer that God would surround the house with protection. The thought of how easily that truck could have taken out Felicity pierced him with an unnerving fear of losing her.

Of failing her, he amended.

When no more noise came from upstairs, Westley heaved a relieved sigh and hoped she would be able to rest after the day she'd had. Being a target of the Red Rose Killer, then discovering the awful truth that her father had been murdered and then someone trying to take her life—it was more than most people could handle in such a short time. Yet, Felicity was strong in spirit and personality. Stronger than he'd ever given her credit for. Her father would be proud of her.

Westley was proud of her. His respect and admiration for her had increased tenfold. How could he go from thinking she was annoying to realizing she was so special? Special and beautiful. Kind and smart.

Just because he was noticing her good qualities didn't mean he had any intention of becoming romantically involved. He wasn't looking for a romance with the pretty staff sergeant.

In fact, any sort of relationship would only end in disaster. He believed that with his whole being.

He wasn't cut out for commitment. He wasn't the kind of guy a woman should pin her hopes on. According to his mother, he had too much of his father in him.

And too much of his mother.

Both were scarred and dysfunctional. Stood to reason that he was damaged goods, too. He'd promised himself long ago he would never saddle another person with his horrible baggage. And the last person he ever wanted to dump his past on was Felicity. She deserved better than the likes of him.

He would protect her with his life.

But he had a sinking feeling protecting his heart wouldn't be as easy.

SEVEN

In the bright morning light that had her squinting, Felicity followed the smell of brewing coffee and spicy sausage into the kitchen. She halted on the threshold.

Her sleep-fogged brain processed the sight of Dakota lying by the back door. He lifted his head from his chew bone and wagged his tail in greeting, while Westley stood at the stove wearing her father's black barbecue apron over his battle-ready pants and a white T-shirt that molded to the hard planes and angles of his chest and back. His dark hair was spiky on top and his strong jaw was shadowed by stubble.

The pull of attraction zinged through her veins. Beneath her fresh battle-ready uniform, a blush warmed her skin.

He glanced her way. Appreciation gleamed in his blue eyes and he flashed her a crooked grin. "Hope you like chorizo and eggs. It's all I could find that was edible in your refrigerator besides salad dressing."

"Smells delicious." Stifling the urge to flip back her hair, she walked to the coffeemaker and poured herself a mug before taking a seat at the counter. "I haven't been shopping in a while."

"We'll remedy that today," he commented as he turned off the flame beneath the fry pan.

Having only seen him eat prepared meals, she said, "I didn't know you cooked."

"I can on occasion." He dished out the steaming scrambled eggs and sausage onto two plates.

"My dad taught me the basics, enough that I can get by." She let out a wry laugh. "I'm still not comfortable with a steak or fish."

"I can show you how to grill a flawless steak or poach a fish to perfection."

Somehow his words didn't strike her as a boast, but were simply a statement of fact. The man knew how to do things.

"That would be great." The idea of him giving her a cooking lesson thrilled her more than she cared to admit. "Did your mother teach you?"

Westley set a plate in front of her along with a fork and stared at her a moment before replying. "One of my foster mothers was a gourmet chef and she made it a point to teach each kid that came through her home how to cook. She made cooking fun and interesting. She let us experiment with food and spices and such."

Absorbing his words, Felicity wasn't sure what to say. Remembering how he'd shut her down yesterday when she'd asked about his father, she hesitated probing further. But then again, he'd volunteered the information. She could hear the fondness in his voice as he spoke of the foster parent who'd taken the time to teach him to cook, but she couldn't help but hurt for his lack of a normal childhood. "How many foster homes were you in?"

Carrying his plate, he came around the island and sat beside her. "Four."

Her hurt for him quadrupled. "How old were you when you entered the system?"

"Ten."

But his father hadn't passed on until Westley was seventeen, she recalled. Obviously, there was more to the story there. Curiosity drove her to ask another question. "What happened to your parents?"

"Let's bless this food and eat it before it gets cold," he said.

She bowed her head. "Dear Lord, bless this food to our bodies and our bodies to Your service. Amen."

When she raised her gaze, she found Westley staring at her.

"My dad's blessing," she explained.

"I like it." He shoveled a forkful of egg and sausage into his mouth.

He wasn't going to make it easy to get him to open up. And for the life of her she couldn't understand why it was so important that he did. Granted, they would be together, close together, for the foreseeable future and she was putting her life in his hands. Trusting him to have her back.

Getting to know each other better seemed logical. Practical. It would deepen the trust between them. But she could be patient. Letting the subject drop for now, she ate, enjoying the heat of the meat-infused eggs.

After her last bite, she sighed with contentment. "My dad would make this combo on Saturday mornings. My mom didn't like the spiciness. But I love it. Thank you so much."

"I guessed as much last night when you asked for extra jalapeños in your tacos. And you're welcome."

She grinned. "I own stock in antacids."

His laugh was rich and deep and shuddered through her with a delicious wave of warmth.

His cell phone rang. He set his fork on his empty plate and excused himself to take the call. He opened the back door, letting Dakota outside while he stepped onto the porch. Felicity could hear the low murmur of his voice as she washed their dishes and the frying pan, then set them on the drying rack next to the sink.

Westley returned to the kitchen. "That was Justin. The meeting has been moved up. We need to get to base command pronto."

"Let me just brush my teeth and I'll be ready to go." She hurried upstairs, forcing from her mind all thoughts of cooking lessons, foster homes and delicious male laughter. She needed to stay focused.

After securing her hair into a regulation braid with the ends tucked out of sight under her beret, she finished getting ready. She paused on the landing to the stairs. Below, Westley had squatted down to Dakota and was rubbing him behind the ears. The dog's eyes practically rolled back into his head with pleasure. Her insides melted a little at the show of affection between dog and man. And some part of her yearned to have that same sort of attention directed to her.

She nearly snorted aloud at the ridiculous thought. *Get a grip*, she told herself. Just because Westley was being nice to her while he was forced to have her underfoot didn't mean she had to go all mushy about him. Still, she couldn't deny the tender feelings growing in her heart. She ached at the thought that he'd grown up in foster care. She wondered why. What had happened to put him in that position?

Patience, she reminded herself. Her father always said she had a gift for getting others to open up. She'd redirected that ability to the dogs while working with them. Eventually, she'd crack Westley's hard shell and work the story out of him. She only hoped she was brave enough to handle whatever she found inside.

Westley held open the door to base command for Felicity to enter before him. Carrying her camera bag over her shoulder, she smiled her thanks to him as she passed to enter the building. She had a great smile that reached her blue-green eyes. Something he'd tried hard in the past not to notice because he'd been her commanding officer.

Right now, though, he let himself take all of her in, including the vanilla scent wafting from her hair. This morning when she'd come downstairs for breakfast she'd worn the long strands loose and swinging before she'd braided it and tucked up under her beret. He liked that she wore a minimal amount of makeup, just enough to highlight her already pretty features.

He gave himself a mental shake as they were ushered into the conference room. He needed to keep his head in the game and ignore the attraction and affection for Felicity building in his chest. He couldn't believe he'd confessed he'd been in foster care. Revealing such intimate details of his past hadn't been intentional, yet talking about the woman who'd taught him to cook to Felicity had come easily. It distressed him how easy a lot of things were with Felicity.

The conference room was filled, every chair at the

table taken. Ian leaned against the wall and nodded in greeting as Westley and Felicity took positions beside him. Base commander Lieutenant General Hall seated at the head of the long table, held up a hand to gain the room's attention.

To the right of the lieutenant general sat FBI agent Oliver Davison and to the lieutenant general's left was Justin. Also seated at the table were Linc, Ethan and several other members of the Security Forces.

Westley was surprised to see Ethan Webb's ex-wife, Jillian Masters, seated at the table as well. She wore her US Marine dress uniform and a scowl on her face. Apparently, she wasn't on base by choice. Westley met Ethan's gaze. The tension in his friend's eyes was palpable.

Also at the table, seated next to Justin, was a pretty redhead dressed in civilian clothes and clearly very pregnant, while a tall, imposing man, also a civilian by the looks of his Western-style jeans and button-down shirt, stood behind her with his hands on the back of her chair.

"Let's get this briefing going," Lieutenant General Hall said. "I'd like to introduce Deputy Sheriff Serena Hargrove and her husband, Jason Hargrove, former Dallas PD. Together with Deputy Hargrove's K-9, they brought down Boyd Sullivan the first go-round."

A murmur rippled through the room. Westley had read the news reports of how the deputy and her K-9 partner, an English springer spaniel trained in wilderness air search, had tracked Boyd to a remote cabin in the Texas Hill Country. He'd like to talk to the officer about her canine and look in to adding the specialized work to the training center. But that would have to wait until life returned to normal. As long as Sullivan was on the loose, Westley's focus was to protect Felicity.

"Deputy, what can you tell us about Boyd?" Lieutenant General Hall asked.

The woman's lips twisted. "He has a sick mind, but make no mistake, he is intelligent and sly. He doesn't do anything without careful planning. And his ego is as big as the State of Texas."

Lieutenant Preston Flanigan, one of the Security Forces members, leaned forward. "How did *you* manage to catch him?"

Preston had been in the last K-9 training session. Westley thought the young cop was a bit too impatient, but hoped the guy would chill eventually. He'd have to if he hoped to be a K-9 handler.

Serena spared him a glance then focused back on Lieutenant General Hall. "Boyd hadn't expected my partner, Ginger. She's small, but mighty. She caught him by surprise and distracted him long enough for me to apprehend him."

"I was there," Oliver said. "I can vouch that Serena and her little dog acted bravely. The arrest was a good one."

"Do you think that's why he messed with the kennels and released all the dogs? Hoped we'd be too busy recovering them to search for him?" Linc said.

Jason Hargrove spoke up. "Having spent more time with Sullivan than I care to ever repeat, I can tell you he believes he can outsmart anyone. I have no doubt he thought the chaos would afford him time and opportunity to move freely."

"Which it did," Justin stated. "Did Boyd have a partner in Dill?"

Serena shook her head. "Not that we know of. There was no indication of one."

Lieutenant General Hall's gaze zeroed on Ian. "What about the cook?"

"The medical examiner says cause of death was strangulation," Ian replied.

"Stephen Butler's ID badge was used to gain access at the south gate at oh-four-hundred," Justin explained. "We're still working on how Boyd got off the base after the attacks."

"Are we sure he left?" Ethan asked. "Just because the news reported sightings of him, we can't know for sure if he's off base or not." His gaze slid to his ex-wife and then away.

Jillian's lips twisted, but the woman made no comment.

Justin nodded. "That's true. Which is why the base is on high alert with extra security at the gates. And Baylor Marine Base is also coordinating their effort with ours to find the escaped prisoner before he hurts anyone else."

Lieutenant General Hall rose. "I want Sullivan found. And the person who is helping him. Am I clear?"

A chorus of "Yes, sir" filled the room.

"Dismissed," Lieutenant General Hall said. He turned to the two civilians. "Thank you for coming all this way."

"I wish we could be more help," the deputy said as her husband helped her to her feet.

Felicity leaned close to whisper in Westley's ear. "We should talk to her about wilderness air-search training."

Having her echo his earlier thought made him grin. "Good idea."

She held his gaze for a moment. Something flared in her eyes before she quickly looked away. A slight pink tinged her cheeks. He wasn't sure what he'd seen. Approval? Attraction? Disconcerted, he pushed aside the thought and followed the Hargroves out of the conference room.

After introducing himself and Felicity, he said, "I would love to hear about the wilderness air-search training you did with your K-9 partner."

"If you give me your contact info, I can put you in touch with the trainer that we used," Serena said.

"I'd appreciate that." He gave her his cell-phone number and email address then bid them goodbye.

Westley escorted Felicity to the photo lab for her new assignment.

"Deputy Hargrove looked like she was uncomfortable," Felicity said. "She has to be close to her due date."

Westley made a noncommittal noise. He didn't know anything about due dates or pregnancies in humans. Dog gestation periods he understood.

Setting her camera bag on an empty desk, Felicity peered at him with curiosity shining in her eyes. "Do you ever think you'll have your own kids?"

"Me?" He nearly choked on the word. "No. What about you?"

She shrugged. "Maybe. If I find the right man to share my life with."

He told himself to forget it. It was none of his business but the words flowed off his tongue before he could stop himself. "Ever been close to walking down the aisle?"

She let out a laugh that was half bitter and half self-effacing. "Hardly." A flicker of hurt crossed her face be-

"4 for 4" MINI-SURVEY

We are prepared to **REWARD** you with 2 FREE books and 2 FREE gifts for completing our MINI SURVEY!

FREE Value Over **$20!**

You'll get...

TWO FREE BOOKS & TWO FREE GIFTS

just for participating in our Mini Survey!

Dear Reader,

IT'S A FACT: if you answer 4 quick questions, we'll send you 4 FREE REWARDS!

I'm not kidding you. As a leading publisher of women's fiction, we value your opinions… and your time. That's why we are prepared to **reward** you handsomely for completing our mini-survey. In fact, we have 4 Free Rewards for you, including 2 free books and 2 free gifts.

As you may have guessed, that's why our mini-survey is called **"4 for 4".** Answer 4 questions and get 4 Free Rewards. It's that simple!

Thank you for participating in our survey,

Pam Powers

To get your 4 FREE REWARDS:
Complete the survey below and return the insert today to receive 2 FREE BOOKS and 2 FREE GIFTS guaranteed!

"4 for 4" MINI-SURVEY

1 Is reading one of your favorite hobbies?
☐ YES ☐ NO

2 Do you prefer to read instead of watch TV?
☐ YES ☐ NO

3 Do you read newspapers and magazines?
☐ YES ☐ NO

4 Do you enjoy trying new book series with FREE BOOKS?
☐ YES ☐ NO

YES! I have completed the above Mini-Survey. Please send me my 4 FREE REWARDS (worth over $20 retail). I understand that I am under no obligation to buy anything, as explained on the back of this card.

☐ I prefer the regular-print edition
153/353 IDL GMYM

☐ I prefer the larger-print edition
107/307 IDL GMYM

FIRST NAME   LAST NAME

ADDRESS

APT.#   CITY

STATE/PROV.   ZIP/POSTAL CODE

Offer limited to one per household and not applicable to series that subscriber is currently receiving.
Your Privacy—The Reader Service is committed to protecting your privacy. Our Privacy Policy is available online at www.ReaderService.com or upon request from the Reader Service. We make a portion of our mailing list available to reputable third parties that offer products we believe may interest you. If you prefer that we not exchange your name with third parties, or if you wish to clarify or modify your communication preferences, please visit us at www.ReaderService.com/consumerschoice or write to us at Reader Service Preference Service, P.O. Box 9062, Buffalo, NY 14240-9062. Include your complete name and address.   SLI-218-MS17

fore she turned away to busy herself unpacking her bag. He didn't like to think some guy had caused her pain.

"Why do you say it like that?"

She shrugged. "I haven't found anyone I click with, I guess. The men I've dated were disappointing." Her lips twisted. "Or rather I was the disappointment. Maybe my expectations are too high."

He couldn't imagine anyone being disappointed in her. She was fun and smart, and pretty. "You have criteria?"

She smiled faintly. "Yes. I want sparks," she said. "I want to be loved as I am. I want to share my faith as well as my life with the man I give my heart to."

"Those sound reasonable," he murmured. He wondered if she felt the sparks that he did whenever they were together. Probably not.

It was best not to let himself put too much stock in his attraction to the lovely sergeant. Their situation was temporary. They both had jobs to do. And when the killers—Boyd and the person who murdered her father—were arrested and locked away, Westley and Felicity would return to the training center and life would resume as before. And if he kept telling himself that eventually he'd make it happen.

She peered at him with curiosity shining in her eyes. "What about you?"

He should have expected the question. His stomach twisted. "Marriage isn't something I plan on tackling."

She frowned. "Why not?"

How could he explain he was afraid his father and mother's pattern of behavior would somehow play out in his life? That he wouldn't ever risk letting anyone close enough to find out?

The door to the photo lab opened and Commander Lieutenant General Hall walked in, saving Westley from replying. Westley and Felicity snapped to attention and saluted.

Lieutenant General Hall returned the salute. "At ease."

Relaxing, Westley moved aside to allow the lieutenant general to address Felicity.

"I see you're settling in," Lieutenant General Hall commented.

"Just starting to, sir," she said.

"You know your assignment?"

"Take as many photos as possible all over base in the hope I capture Boyd's image," she replied. "Or his interest."

Westley's gut clenched at her words. He'd be with her, by her side to protect her, but it didn't make stomaching the fact that she was being dangled out like a piece of squid to hook a shark any more appealing.

Lieutenant General Hall clapped her on the shoulder. "You've got heart, Staff Sergeant Monroe. Your father would be very proud of you."

Surprise marched across her face before her expression softened. "Thank you, sir. That means a lot to me."

Westley wondered why she always appeared amazed when anyone mentioned her father's pride in her.

"Sir, I'd like to carry a service weapon," Felicity said.

Lieutenant General Hall frowned. "Only Security Forces personnel are allowed to carry on base. It would raise too many questions if the base photographer carried."

Westley sensed her frustration. He could appreciate

her need to have a sidearm. But she would have to be content to have him and Dakota at her side.

"Master Sergeant James," Lieutenant General Hall said, focusing his eagle-eyed gaze on Westley. "I trust you and your dog will keep Staff Sergeant Monroe from harm?"

Squaring his shoulders, Westley met Lieutenant General Hall with a level gaze. "Of course, sir. With our lives."

Westley heard Felicity's sharp inhale but he kept his attention on Lieutenant General Hall.

"Very good. Keep my office informed and be careful." Lieutenant General Hall left the room.

Once the door closed, Felicity stepped close and scrutinized him with a pinched brow. "Did you mean that?"

He blinked, unsure what she referred to. Was she jumping back to their conversation about marriage? "Excuse me?"

"That you'd protect me with your life?"

Relieved by the question, he nodded. "Absolutely."

Looking pleased, she grabbed her camera. "Then we'd best get to it."

Felicity had been the base photographer for two days and she loved it. Some of the photos would be used for PR, others for the base newsletter, website and social media.

She loved the freedom to roam unfettered, to capture moments that might otherwise go unnoticed. Loved the joy of not having to be exacting with the lighting and the composition of the shots, but rather catching unposed, unscripted action shots of airmen going about their day, or contemplative images of the various personnel across the expanse of the base.

And having Westley and Dakota at her side, knowing they had her back, allowed her to focus on the camera.

They stopped at the edge of the training obstacle course, where a basic military-training unit ran through the obstacles. She adjusted the f-stop and clicked off a multitude of shots. And she knew that some were spectacular. Not all, but there would be some she'd be proud of. Over the last two days it seemed she'd taken more pictures than she had her whole life. The SD card was nearly full. They'd taken a few breaks to eat lunch, to let Dakota rest and to use the facilities. Soon they would stop for the day and head back to base command.

A gust of wind whipped her hair into her eyes. Her braid had completely fallen apart over an hour ago, so she'd tied her hair back with a rubber band, but the ends were still giving her grief in the Texas breeze.

"Here. Hold this." She handed her camera to Westley so she could free up her hands. Then she adjusted the strap of her camera bag across her body into a more comfortable position.

After securing her hair into a bun at her nape, she took the camera back and lifted the lens to her eye, clicking through more shots. Something in the background moved in the woods beyond the young airmen. She zoomed in.

A tan dog peeked out from around the trunk of a tree. Her heart rate ticked up. "Westley, there's a Belgian about forty meters straight out behind the tree with the crooked top."

She handed him the camera so he could use the lens to see what she had. "Niko."

Taking the camera back, she said, "You should go get him."

"*We'll* go get him," he countered. "Come on."

Inordinately pleased by his inclusion of her even though she knew he simply wanted her near for her safety, she jogged with him and Dakota to the wooded area that made up the back part of the base.

Westley whistled, catching the dog's attention. "Niko. Come."

The dog hesitated. Felicity was afraid the dog would bolt. From her camera bag she grabbed the banana she'd taken from the commissary at lunch. She unpeeled the fruit and then broke off a piece. Holding it in her hand so that it was visible to the dog, she dangled it low against her thigh. "Come. Treat."

Niko's nose twitched, then he was loping toward her, clearly wanting the offered banana. As soon as his mouth touched the fruit, Westley grabbed Niko's collar.

Westley met her gaze. "Well done."

She blinked. For a moment her old defenses rose, making her wonder if he was mocking her after the tirade she'd heaped on his head about being stingy with his praise, but his expression was open and his approval appeared genuine. She grinned. "Thank you."

Westley threaded Dakota's lead through Niko's collar so the two dogs were tied together. "Let's get this guy to the vet and make sure he's okay."

They loaded the dogs into Westley's vehicle and drove to the other side of the base. The vet checked out the dog and declared him slightly dehydrated but otherwise in good health. Felicity was thankful. She worried about the remaining missing dogs and prayed they would be found soon.

"They'll start making their way back. Just like Niko did," Westley told her as if he sensed her anxious thoughts.

Strange that in such a short time they would be so connected, she thought. "I'm sure you're right."

After dropping Niko off with Caleb at the training center and feeding Dakota dinner, Felicity was anxious to get the photos uploaded so she could go home and put her feet up.

Once they arrived back at base command, she made quick work of uploading the images and sending them to the FBI database. As she settled into the passenger seat of Westley's vehicle, she yawned.

"Don't fall asleep on me yet," Westley told her. "We've got to go to the BX and buy some more groceries."

She groaned. "Can't we order something to go?"

He let out a scoffing laugh. "I have a feeling you do that often."

"It's easier," she admitted. Most nights she was too tired to bother with making her own food.

"Fine. How about a hamburger and fries?"

"I'll take a hamburger and a salad," she countered.

They drove to the nearest burger joint located near the BX, ordered and headed back to her house. He unpacked the takeout bag while she filled glasses with water and snagged her favorite salad dressing from the refrigerator. Westley blessed their meal, and then dug in to his burger and fries.

She shook the bottle of dressing before pouring a generous amount over the lettuce and assorted vegetables.

Westley raised an eyebrow. "Drowning your greens, huh?"

A low rumble emanated from Dakota's throat. His gaze was on Felicity. She made a face. "What's he doing?"

"I don't know," Westley said. "Dakota, sit."

The dog continued to stare at her while he obeyed the command.

Stabbing her fork into the salad, she took a bite.

Dakota barked and jumped onto the table. Using his nose, he knocked her salad to the floor, making a huge mess.

"Hey!" she protested.

Dakota put his nose to Felicity's mouth and whined. She held herself still, unsure what was happening. Would the dog attack? She couldn't wrap her mind around his strange behavior.

Westley scrambled out of his chair and grabbed Dakota by the collar and yanked him to the floor. "I've never seen him do that before."

Felicity's stomach roiled. Sweat broke out across her body. "I'm going to be sick."

She clamped a hand over her mouth and swallowed convulsively.

"Felicity!"

She heard Westley's voice, heard the panic, the fear, but she couldn't respond as the world titled, swam out of focus. She listed to the side, sliding off the chair onto the floor, but the impact barely registered. Her mind screamed a warning. Something was wrong. Very, very wrong.

EIGHT

Heart pounding in his ears, Westley dove to his knees beside Felicity where she'd fallen to the kitchen floor. Dakota whined. He'd dropped to his belly, his nose stretched out to Felicity.

Her eyes were closed. Westley couldn't tell if she was breathing.

Please, Lord. I can't take another death.

Lungs frozen in dread, he pressed his fingers against the tender skin of her neck. He felt the steady thrum of her pulse beating there. She was alive. The tight vise that had gripped his chest expanded, allowing him to breathe. Had she had a seizure? That would explain Dakota's behavior. Some dogs had the uncanny ability to sense an oncoming seizure. Westley had never seen it happen and hadn't known Dakota was that sensitive.

He yanked his phone from his pocket and dialed 911. He quickly explained to the dispatcher the issue and gave the address. Keeping the line open, he set down the phone and placed a hand to Felicity's cheek. Her skin was clammy.

The pungent odor of the salad dressing invaded his senses. His mind replayed the scene in his head. Dakota had acted strange immediately after Felicity had opened the dressing bottle. If the dog's disobedience wasn't enough, he'd attacked her salad bowl, sending it flying.

A knot of apprehension twisted in Westley's gut. His gaze flew to the dressing bottle still standing on the dining table. Had the contents been tampered with? Had Dakota picked up a deadly scent?

Fear sidled up and choked him.

The sound of sirens rent the air. He jumped to his feet and ran to the front door, opening it wide and urging the paramedics inside.

"She's got a pulse but it's weak," he told them. "I think she may have been poisoned."

"Westley?" Justin rushed to his side. "I heard the call come in."

Glad to have his captain's support, Westley told him what had happened while the paramedics tended to Felicity. "The dressing. It needs to be tested for poison."

"I'll take care of it and Dakota," Justin said. "You go with Felicity."

Westley nodded and hustled after the paramedics as they loaded Felicity into the back bay of the ambulance. Taking a seat on the bench next to her, he took her hand. "Felicity, stay with me, okay?"

She looked so vulnerable lying there with an oxygen mask covering half her face. He hated seeing her like this. He wanted her to wake up and chew him out again. He wanted to see her smile and hear her laugh. Feelings he'd been trying to contain bubbled up, escaping the compartment he'd stuffed them into. If he was being honest with himself, he would admit that he'd grown to care for the young staff sergeant. No, *care* wasn't the right word. He was falling for her in ways that terrified him. He lifted her hand to his lips and kissed her knuckles. She had to be okay.

He bowed his head and silently prayed like he'd never prayed before.

At the hospital, Felicity was whisked away behind the closed doors of the emergency room. Westley was barred from following. He paced the waiting area as frustration and fear spiraled through him.

He spotted First Lieutenant Vanessa Gomez at the nurses' station and rushed over. "Lieutenant Gomez."

"Master Sergeant James." She acknowledged his salute. "Can I help you?"

"Yes." He told her about Felicity. "Can you check on her? Please?"

"Of course." Concern laced Vanessa's voice. Without another word, she hurried through the swinging door and disappeared.

An interminable amount of time ticked by as Westley continued to pace until Vanessa finally returned. "Dr. Knight will be out shortly to talk to you."

"Is she…" He couldn't get the words to come out.

"They are working on her." Compassion shone in her eyes. "You have to trust she'll be okay."

He nodded. He wanted to trust that God would save her. Westley hated the feeling of helplessness stealing over him.

Finally, a doctor in a white lab coat approached. The name tag on his breast pocket read Dr. Trevor Knight. "Are you Master Sergeant James?"

"Yes." Westley's heart stuttered as he waited to hear the news. "How is Felicity?"

"She's going to be fine," Trevor assured him. "Be-cause of the suspected poison, we administered activated charcoal and pumped fluids to flush her system. We heard from Security Forces that the tainted salad dressing contained crushed hemlock leaves. Very toxic and fast-acting. If you hadn't reacted swiftly…" The doctor didn't say it, but Westley knew the potential outcome. "But the staff sergeant ingested such a small amount that there shouldn't be any residual after-effects."

"Thank you." Palpable relief coursed through Westley's veins. "When can I see her?"

"She's resting now, but you're welcome to sit with her," Trevor said. "Follow me."

He led Westley to a private room. Felicity was lying in the bed, a blanket tucked around her as she slept. Her loose, light brown hair spilled over the pillow, making his mouth dry. He moved to sit beside the bed and brushed a few stray strands of hair from her face. Dark lashes rested against her cheeks.

He took her hand, so soft and warm, and settled back to wait for her to wake up, though he had no idea how to proceed from here. He'd grown attached to this beautiful, spirited woman. But how could he ever act on his feelings when doing so would jeopardize both of their careers in the air force? No, he had to find a way to stuff his emotions back into their boxes and maintain a professional distance from Felicity.

Unfortunately, he had a feeling that might be as easy as bottling her laughter.

"You're going to be okay."

Felicity pressed her lips together to keep a chuckle from escaping. From the moment she'd awoken in the hospital with Westley holding her hand, he'd been comforting, soothing, and had assured her that she hadn't ingested enough of the poison inside the tainted bottle of salad dressing to cause any permanent damage. "So you've said for at least the tenth time."

After being discharged, Westley had brought her home and insisted she rest on the couch. He'd put an afghan over her, fluffed a pillow behind her head and brought her a tall glass of water.

She should be annoyed by his incessant need to treat her like an invalid except the relief, concern and tenderness in his eyes made her heart pound. She couldn't deny she liked having his attention, the good kind, lavished on her. He made her feel special and cared for. His haggard appearance was testament to having slept by her bedside in the hospital last night. Only a man who cared would do that, right?

She had no idea what to do with the thought, so she tucked it away for safekeeping.

"Sorry. I'm hovering." He frowned, clearly befuddled by his own behavior.

She captured his hand and gave a gentle squeeze. "It's all right. I'm sure it was scary. I'm grateful for Dakota or I'd have kept eating the salad."

"He's a hero."

She turned her focus to the dog in question. He sat next to the couch with his nose resting on her knee. "You're a good boy, Dakota."

His tail wagged.

"He must have smelled the hemlock in the dressing," she said.

"A good thing, too. His sensitive nose saved your life."

She'd seen dogs turn away from tainted food before, that wasn't something that needed to be trained into a dog. She was glad that Dakota was watching out for her welfare.

The house phone rang. Westley brought her the cordless handset. She glanced at the caller ID and sighed inwardly when she saw it was Dr. Flintman, the base therapist. No doubt he'd heard about her trip to the ER. "Hello."

"Felicity," the doctor's deep, kind voice boomed in her ear. She held the phone slightly away from her. "You haven't been in to see me."

She smiled wryly. "No. I've been a bit busy."

"I've heard. Very traumatic. How are you coping? Are you still having nightmares?"

She could honestly say she hadn't had one for the past few nights. First, because she'd felt safe with Westley downstairs, and then, of course, last night was spent in the hospital. "I'm doing okay. I haven't had a nightmare in a few days."

"Hmm. You really should come in to the office. I have some medication I think will help to keep you doing okay."

"Like I said before, I'd rather not take anything. If things get bad again, I'll call."

"Well, I can't make you, but I'm here if you need me." The doctor hung up.

Felicity placed the handset on the end table and met Westley's curious gaze. He'd taken a seat in her father's recliner. It was nice to see him sitting there. Her father wouldn't have minded.

"Nightmares?" Westley asked.

She'd been worried that Westley would find out about her visits to the base therapist. Now, though, she had no choice but to tell him the truth and hope he wouldn't think differently of her. "After I found my father, I started having really bad dreams. I sought help with Dr. Flintman."

"Ah. Good for you."

The approval in his eyes pleased her, and she felt relieved. "It helped a bit to talk about it. He offered to prescribe some medication that he thought I'd benefit from but I'm holding off taking it."

"I understand. But if things get bad—"

"I'll reconsider," she said.

"Okay." He leaned back. "Lieutenant General Hall said you are to rest today and we'll get back to work tomorrow."

"Did you sleep at all?"

"No."

Tender empathy crowded her chest. "I think we could both use the rest." She rubbed Dakota's head. "We've got an alarm right here." She could tell Westley wanted to protest. "Please."

He nodded. "I won't be any good if I'm asleep on my feet." He pulled the lever that elevated his feet and reclined the chair back. He cocked an eyebrow. "Aren't you going to rest, too?"

She did chuckle then. "Yes, I will."

She stretched out on the couch and turned on her side to face him. After a moment, she closed her eyes, sure she wouldn't fall asleep with him so close by.

But it was two hours later when a pounding noise woke her up. Her eyes popped open in time to see Westley vault from the recliner, his hand on his sidearm. He blinked several times as if getting his bearing.

Sitting up, she said, "Someone is at the front door."

He strode across the living room and pulled open the door. Tech Sergeant Linc Colson stood there.

"The captain asked me to swing by and check on you two," Linc stated.

Westley stepped aside so he could enter. "We were resting."

Linc came all the way into the living room. "It's good to see you're doing well," he said to Felicity.

"Thanks." Deciding this would be a good time to freshen up, she stood up. "I'm going upstairs."

Westley hurried to her side as she headed to the staircase. She leveled him with a pointed look. "I don't need you hovering."

He raised his hands. "My bad."

She couldn't resist touching a hand to his chest. "You're a good man, Westley James."

His blue eyes darkened with something that made her pulse skip. She jerked her hand back and fled upstairs before she gave in to the dangerous urge to kiss him.

It took all of Westley's self-control not to chase her upstairs and tug her into his arms and kiss her. He'd seen the yearning on her pretty face and felt the answering longing deep inside of himself. If they'd been alone…

Wow. He was in so much trouble.

Kissing Felicity would be…amazing. Not to mention reckless.

And knowing that she'd felt it, too, sent joy soaring through him. He quickly wrestled the wayward attraction into a far corner where it wouldn't see the light of day again. Or at least where he could pretend it didn't exist.

He had to keep his head and his heart on the path before him. Logically, he understood his emotions were heightened from nearly losing her. They were both running on intensified feelings that had no place in their world.

Linc's rumbling laughter tightened Westley's shoulder muscles. A flush of embarrassment heated his face. He couldn't remember ever feeling so... He wasn't even sure what the term for it was. Vulnerable? Out of control?

Calming his racing emotions, he turned to face his friend. "What are you chuckling about?"

"You." He gestured to the stairs with his chin. "And her."

"I have no idea what you mean." Westley walked into the kitchen and poured himself a glass of tap water. He drank it as though he'd been stranded in the desert. The cool liquid helped to center his thoughts. His job was to protect Felicity, not pant after her like a lovesick teen. "Help me throw out every scrap of food in the house. I don't know what else might have been tampered with and I won't take any chances with her life."

"Why don't we have the crime-scene techs test everything?"

"It will be more expedient to just clear out the cupboards and fridge, then start over with sealed goods."

"Why would Boyd Sullivan put poison in her food?" Linc shook his head. "It doesn't fit."

Westley contemplated telling Linc about Agent Monroe's murder. Not that he didn't trust his friend, but Westley decided it would be best to keep that information in a close circle. Less chance to tip off the murderer that way.

"Do you think you two should even stay here?" Linc asked.

"I don't know if she'll leave." Westley spread his hands. "Besides, where would we go?" It occurred to him he'd automatically included himself. But for now they were a package deal. Until the threat to her life was neutralized, he wasn't leaving her side.

"There's base housing near the command center."

"I'll talk to her about it." He tossed a box of cereal into the garbage can. "How is the investigation coming? I assume Sullivan hasn't been found or I'd have heard."

"Unfortunately, we're no closer to catching him than we were yesterday. But we do have a lead."

That comment raised the hair at his nape. "What do you mean?"

"Someone is revealing information about the investigation to an anonymous blogger. Information that we haven't made public and weren't intending to."

"That sounds dangerous." Westley thought for a moment. "Could it be one of the base reporters? They've been sniffing around, asking questions, showing up everywhere."

Linc shrugged. "Maybe. Whoever the person is revealed that Zoe Sullivan visited her half brother just two weeks before his escape. Very few people knew that bit of info. Now the base is speculating she's helping her brother."

"Do you think she is?"

"I'm not sure, but I'm keeping an eye on her. She's cagey. Something's definitely up with her. Frankly, I don't trust anyone related by blood or friendship to Boyd Sullivan."

"I don't blame you there," Westley said. "Although innocent until proven guilty."

"Right." Linc checked his watch. "Hey, I have to go. Zoe's teaching a class and it ends soon. We can't have her walking around base unattended."

"Be careful," Westley told him.

Felicity stepped into the kitchen, blocking Linc's path, and looked at Westley. "What are you two doing?"

Westley paused with a bag of spaghetti hovering over the garbage can. She looked so pretty wearing jeans and a long-sleeve button-down top in a kelly green that deepened the color of her eyes. She'd twisted her hair at the back of her head, exposing the creamy column of her neck. But it was her eyes that caught his attention, eyes that sparked a warning he was beginning to know—and appreciate—well.

"Getting rid of any more potential hazards to your health," he stated and dropped the spaghetti into the garbage.

"I guess that's the best thing to do." She reached up to finger the key hanging around her neck.

Linc peered closer at the key. "You ride?"

"Ride what?" she asked.

He pointed at the key dangling from the chain. "That's a key to a BMW 2-series motorcycle. Vintage. Probably late sixties."

"Are you sure?" Westley exchanged a glance with Felicity. The hit-and-run her father had been investigating involved a motorcycle. Could they have the key to the one that hit the pedestrian? Literally the key to a big chunk of the mystery?

"Yes." Linc shrugged. "I like motorcycles. Do you

have the bike? It would be worth some money. A collector's item."

She tucked the key inside her blouse. "No. Just a memento."

"Ah. Well, I'm outta here." He shook Westley's hand. "Let me know if you need anything."

"We will." Westley walked him to the living room door. "Thanks, man."

As soon as the door closed behind Linc, Felicity said, "Did you hear that?" Anticipation echoed in her tone.

"Let's not get too hopeful," he said. "Even if that is the key to the motorcycle that your father was investigating, we still have no clue where it could be stashed."

"True. We need to get back out there," she said.

"Tomorrow is soon enough."

She nodded. "You're right. You know, I've been thinking. We never did search the attic. Maybe Dad's files are there."

"Are you up for it?"

"I am. The rest helped."

"Let's do it." Abandoning the kitchen, they rushed upstairs, stopping beneath the attic access door with a step stool she'd retrieved from her father's room.

Placing it under the hatch in the ceiling, he climbed up and lifted the door. Grasping the lip, he pulled himself up then reached down to lift her through the opening. The unfinished space ran the length of the house. Rafters provided support for the pitched roof. And stacked boxes provided many places where her father could have hidden his files.

"Most of this is my mom's stuff," Felicity said. "After the divorce, Dad put everything she'd left behind up here."

"Is this going to be painful for you?" Westley asked. He knew the agony of having to deal with the remains of a parent's things. After his father had gone to prison, his mother had tasked him with the job of packing away his dad's things. Westley had refused, which had earned him a beating, ironically with one of his father's belts. Despite the lashing, he hadn't touched his father's belongings.

"I don't think so," she replied. "It will be harder to pack up my dad's things."

His gut clenched. "Yes, it will." He'd admired and envied the love between Felicity and her father.

She lifted the flaps of a box to rummage inside. "Was it hard for you to deal with your father's possessions?"

"Hardly," he said. He moved a box closer to her to look through. He didn't feel comfortable searching through her mother's stuff. He doubted they'd find anything up here. All the boxes had layers of undisturbed dust.

"Will you tell me what happened to him?"

He really didn't want to. Dredging up the past wouldn't serve any purpose. But maybe if he told her, then he wouldn't have to worry about her falling for him. Once she knew the type of gene pool he came from, she'd want to keep far away from him.

"My father was a murderer."

NINE

She couldn't have heard him right. A murderer? Unease slid down Felicity's spine. She inhaled the musty odor of the attic, taking in some dust, and coughed. Catching her breath, she asked, "What happened?"

He sat on a trunk and dropped his head into his hands. There was a long moment of silence. She waited, hoping he would let down his walls and fully open up. He couldn't leave her hanging with such a shocking revelation.

"It was my fault."

His despondent tone broke her heart. She absorbed the blow. "Help me understand."

He lifted his gaze to meet hers. Torment swirled in the blue depths of his eyes. "I was ten when it happened."

So young.

"We were in a busy restaurant," he continued, his gaze dropping to his boots. "My feet were big. Too big. I was awkward, gangly even."

She couldn't imagine him clumsy and self-conscious. When Westley ran alongside the dogs during training he was nimble, but his six-foot frame contained the same sort of coiled power the dogs had. Unlike Felicity, who had cornered the market on gawkiness.

"I tripped over my feet, knocking a man's drink into his lap. He said something harsh to me and my dad took exception." Westley let out a mirthless laugh, a sound she didn't understand.

"They got in a fight. Dad punched the guy hard, he went down and hit his head on the metal foot of the table and died."

Her stomach knotted. What a horrible incident for a child to witness.

"My dad had a long rap sheet for assault and battery so the judge gave him a ten-year sentence for first-degree manslaughter. He died when I was seventeen."

Stunned, she reached out to touch his arm. "I'm sorry."

He shook his head, stopping her from touching him. "No reason for you to be sorry. He was a hothead who couldn't control his anger. It landed him in prison, where there were bigger, angrier men. I'm just surprised it took so long before someone beat him to a pulp."

The breath left her lungs. His callous words echoed with an underpinning of unfathomable pain. She'd had no idea Westley had a traumatic past. And she had no words of comfort to offer. The urge to wrap her arms around him and hold on tight gripped her, but doing so wasn't a good idea for either of them. They had to maintain a professional demeanor if they hoped to work together at the training center in the future. A future where, God willing, the Red Rose Killer was once again behind bars and her father's murderer would be brought to justice.

Despite her warning, she moved closer to sit beside

him and put a hand on his strong shoulder, now bowed with undeserved guilt. He made a distressed sound, as if her offer of comfort hurt him. Her hand floated to her lap.

A thought intruded as she recalled his earlier reaction to remembering the event that led to his father's incarceration and a cold sweat broke out over her skin. "Was your father violent with you? With your mother?"

He stood and paced away. "He was rough. On both of us."

Her heart contracted painfully in her chest with empathy and sorrow. Was that why Westley was so self-contained and unwilling to show emotion? The man had rarely smiled in the six months she'd been under his command. Not for her lack of trying. She'd assumed all this time he was displeased to have her in the training center. Could it be his attitude was more of a shield he hid behind rather than a reflection of his feelings for her?

She'd have to process this at another time. Right now, with him looking like he'd rather be anywhere but here, she sought to ease the hurt stirring within him. "You can't blame yourself for something that was out of your control. You were a child. They were grown men who made the choice to fight."

"Logically, I know that, but that doesn't stop my mother from blaming me. It's why she left. Why I was sent to live in foster care."

The injustice of it all made her so sad and angry that she couldn't ignore her emotions. Professional demeanor could take a flying leap. She went to him and put her arms around his waist. He tensed, holding himself ramrod-straight, his stiff arms at his sides. Frustration pulsed through her. He'd offered her comfort when she'd needed it, yet refused to take it from her.

"Westley," she said, her tone half plea, half censure.

The tension suddenly drained from him and he wrapped his arms around her, drawing her closer. She laid her cheek against his chest. His aftershave—spicy, woodsy and masculine—teased her senses. His heart thudded in time to her own.

His strong arms made her feel safe, cherished even. It was a feeling she could get used to if she allowed herself. She should step back, break the contact before her emotions got too tangled up with him. But she had no willpower. Nor the desire to step away.

He used the crook of his finger to lift her chin and draw her gaze to his. The tenderness in his eyes made her breath hitch, but it was the flare of attraction she saw in them that sent her pulse skyrocketing.

He dipped his head but halted inches from her lips, giving her the choice.

She didn't have to think about it. She wanted him to kiss her. Had for so long, even though she would never have admitted it to anyone, least of all to herself.

Had her former irritation and annoyance with Westley been more about an attraction she hadn't wanted to acknowledge?

Deciding to stay in the moment rather than analyze the past, she rose on her toes, closing the gap, and pressed her mouth to his. His lips were warm and firm, yet so gentle.

One hand stayed at the small of her back, while his other cupped the back of her head.

A low growl filled her head. It took a moment for her to register the sound. Dakota. They'd left him on guard duty in the hall beneath the attic opening. Was he protesting being left out?

Westley drew back. Their gazes met, and questions ricocheted through her mind. What did the kiss mean? Did she want it to mean something? Did he?

Dakota's growl turned into a bark of alarm, sending apprehension cascading over her limbs.

Westley nudged her behind him and leaned cautiously over the side of the attic opening. Unwilling to be coddled, Felicity dropped to her knees beside him to see for herself what had upset the dog. The hall was empty, but Dakota faced her father's room, his tail erect, his ears back and teeth bared, guarding them from an unseen threat.

Westley grabbed Felicity's elbow and tugged her behind him as he reached for the weapon holstered at his thigh. "Stay here."

In a move that was both athletic and fluid, he dropped quickly through the attic opening, landing soundlessly beside Dakota. Frustrated to be sidelined again, Felicity watched the pair advance down the hall, two warriors on the hunt. Dakota's growls and barks bounced off the walls.

Felicity's fingers curled into a fist. Adrenaline pumped through her veins. She needed a weapon.

She'd understood Lieutenant General Hall's refusal to let her carry. It would draw attention to her and make Boyd less likely to attack. Not that Westley and Dakota weren't enough of a deterrent. At the moment, she could only pray for Westley's safety.

Dakota erupted in a barrage of vicious barking.

"Halt!" Westley's shout came from her father's bedroom.

The sound of several gunshots rang out. A canine yelp punctuated the air.

Felicity's heart jackknifed. "Westley!"

Fearing the worst, she scrambled out of the attic, landing ungracefully with a jarring thud on the carpeted hall floor. As she regained her balance, she sent up a prayer, asking God for Westley and Dakota to be all right.

Cautiously, she made her way to the entrance of her father's bedroom, pressing her back against the wall. Anxiety clogged her throat, her mind already preparing her for devastation. She flashed back to the day she found her father's motionless body, and a shudder of dread worked over her flesh. With air trapped in her lungs, she peered around the doorjamb.

Inside the room, she found Westley holding Dakota, praising him with soothing words and a gentle tone. The dog panted at a fast clip. She hurried to their side. "What happened?"

"The intruder got away," he said. "I nicked him in the arm. But Dakota's been hit." His voice shook with emotion. "There's so much blood I can't tell how bad it is."

Her gaze lurched to where Westley's hand gripped Dakota's hind end. Crimson blood seeped through his fingers. She grabbed a pillow from the bed and stripped off the case. "Here." She shoved the wadded-up material at him. "Use this and apply pressure. We have to get him to the vet clinic."

He took the pillowcase and pressed it against Dakota's wound. "Dakota managed to get a piece of the intruder's pant leg."

She followed his gaze to a ragged-edged piece of dark cotton material lying on the carpet.

"Now we at least have his scent as well as his DNA." He gestured to the windowsill, where a smear of blood marred the white molding. "We'll call Security Forces, but right now we have to get Dakota to the vet." He rose, lifting the dog in his arms. "Call Dr. Roark and tell him we're coming."

Worry for Dakota churned in her gut as she made the call to the vet, who promised to be ready for them.

She prayed Dakota's injury was only a flesh wound as she hurried ahead of Westley and opened the front door.

"You drive," Westley said, heading to her car. "I'll hold him."

As soon as she got in the car she placed a call to Security Forces, and someone assured her they'd be at her house promptly to collect the evidence.

The short drive to the clinic seemed to take forever. When they arrived, the doors to the veterinarian hospital wing of the training center were open and Captain Kyle Roark, DVM and head of Canine Veterinary Services at CAFB, stepped out along with a female tech dressed in green scrubs.

"Follow me to exam room three," Dr. Roark said briskly and led the way.

Inside the room, Westley placed Dakota on the metal exam table. The dog tried to stand. Felicity jumped to subdue him at the same time as Westley. Their hands tangled together as they maneuvered Dakota successfully to his uninjured side.

"Good job, you two," Dr. Roark said. "You make a good team."

Felicity's cheeks heated. She met Westley's gaze, noting the appreciation in his eyes.

"Let's see what we have here," the vet said. "You two keep him still while Airman Fielding and I tend to his wound."

As the vet and the tech washed the wound, Felicity leaned in to Dakota's ear. "You're going to be okay."

The dog turned his head and licked her face. A good sign, she hoped.

"Well, now," the vet said. "Looks worse than it is."

She was so thankful to hear those words, Felicity's knees weakened. She could see the pronouncement had the same effect on Westley.

"The bullet grazed his upper thigh. He'll need a couple of stitches but he'll be right as the Texas rain within no time at all."

"That's good to hear, Doc." Westley's voice was filled with relief and gratitude. The lines of worry etched around his mouth eased.

"Airman Fielding will give you detailed instructions on how to care for the wound and a bottle of pain relievers," Dr. Roark said when he was finished administering to the dog. He clapped Westley on the back. "You all should get some rest."

"We will. Thanks." Westley picked up Dakota, cradling him to his chest.

Felicity took the instructions and the meds from the vet tech and then followed Westley outside. "Do you think we should take him to the training center instead of my house?" she asked.

He nodded. "He'll be comfortable in his kennel. And it will keep him from popping a stitch."

Westley headed toward the door that would take them through the back of the center. They entered the kennel room and a barrage of barking ensued. Most of the crates were filled with dogs. The empty ones made her stomach knot. There were still many dogs missing.

She quickly commanded, "Quiet" and the dogs in their kennels obeyed. She was sad to see Riff's crate still empty. She hoped the young Belgian Malinois would be found unharmed.

"You and I will stay here with Dakota," Westley said as he placed the dog gently into a crate and shut the door. "I think it would be safer for all of us."

"I agree," she said, hating to think the intruder might return to her house.

"There's a room here with a cot. We'll take shifts sleeping."

Not the most comfortable situation. But better than the alternative.

"Tomorrow we can figure out new housing," Westley said.

"We can take my uncle up on his offer to stay with him."

"That's one idea," Westley replied.

She chose to let his noncommittal answer go. "Obviously the guy hasn't found what he was looking for." She fingered the key beneath her uniform. "We need to find the motorcycle the key belongs to. Then we'll find my father's killer."

He brushed a stray strand of hair off her cheek, causing a shiver to trip over her skin. She had to look frightful. Just as he did with his uniform smeared with blood. Yet he looked at her like he approved of what he saw. "First things first. Your safety is my priority."

She'd never been anyone's priority. Her mother had been too busy with her law practice and her father too dedicated to the OSI. She'd always felt like an afterthought, unless of course she messed up, then she got their attention. Not the kind of attention she wanted growing up. She liked the idea of being Westley's priority way more than she probably should.

"Let's get back to your house and see how the crime-scene techs are doing." He stepped back. "And you can pack a bag."

They left the training center after checking in with Caleb Streeter, who promised to look in on Dakota. When they arrived at her house, the crime-scene techs were packing up their things and Special Agent Ian Steffen was on scene.

When he saw Felicity he hurried down the walkway, intercepting them. "I was worried about you two." He gave them each a once-over. "I take it neither of you has sustained injuries."

"No, we're good," Westley replied.

"We were in the attic when Dakota alerted us to the intruder," she told him.

Ian's eyebrows rose. "Did you find anything related to the case your father was working on?"

"Unfortunately, no," Westley responded.

But Felicity had learned more about Westley and her own feelings, so not a total loss.

"But hopefully the evidence collected will reveal the intruder's identity," Ian said. "If it was Boyd then we'll know for sure he's still on base."

Felicity didn't believe this was the work of the Red Rose Killer. "We think the intruder was looking for this key." She slipped it from the collar of her uniform.

"Maybe." Ian frowned.

She didn't understand why he refused to consider the key as important. "We have it on good authority that this is a specific type of motorcycle key. Possibly the motorcycle used in the hit-and-run."

That grabbed his attention. "If that is the case, then I should take it for safekeeping."

"But you're not officially working her father's murder," Westley stated. "Won't there be questions if you log the key into evidence for a nonexistent case?"

"I can handle that," Ian said.

"We'll keep the key," Westley said flatly.

Did Westley not trust Ian?

"I'll open an official investigation as soon as I can." Ian's tone held a note of defensiveness.

Westley's hands fisted at his side. "We have to find this guy now. Not later."

"Right now all available resources are on the Red Rose Killer case," Ian said. "That's why you have been detailed to Felicity's protection."

"Last report we heard, Boyd's not on base," Felicity said.

"There have been sightings in multiple places at multiple times. It's like sorting sand for a specific granule," Ian replied, sounding harassed. "The sightings could be to confuse us. To keep us from looking on base."

She could only imagine the pressure Ian was under. They all felt it to some degree.

"Plus, we're working on ferreting out Boyd's accomplice. Interviewing every single person on base, double-checking alibis and looking for any connections to Boyd." Ian wiped a hand over his jaw. "The more time goes by, the more the trail goes cold. Everyone is on high alert." He pinned her with his gaze. "We had the photos you've taken analyzed. But there's no sign of Boyd."

Felicity's stomached knotted. Her priorities were

split between justice for her father and helping to capture the serial killer. "I'll be ready to resume taking pictures tomorrow," she promised.

Westley put his hand on her shoulder. "You were poisoned. If you need more time, you'll take it."

The gruff tone would have set her defenses on edge in the past, but she'd come to realize his default mode when struggling with his emotions. Stifling the urge to give him a reassuring smile, she simply said, "I'm feeling fine."

"Then I'll see you both tomorrow," Ian interjected. "Be safe."

When Ian got into his vehicle and left, Felicity turned to face Westley. "You don't completely trust him, do you?"

Westley shrugged. "I'm not sure what to think. He claims to want to catch your father's killer yet…he's not acting like the threat to your life is important."

"I don't believe that's true. With Boyd Sullivan on the loose, the OSI is stretched thin. Ian has no way to prove my father was murdered. And he's counting on you to protect me."

The skepticism in his eyes said he wasn't convinced. "Which I will," he assured her.

"I know." And that pleased her to no end.

They went inside the house. He followed her to her bedroom, where he inspected her corkboard, which was filled with photos and memorabilia, while she packed a duffel bag with a few days' worth of clothes. She didn't know how long they would stay at the training center, or if they'd move to her uncle's or other base housing.

"You were a cute kid," Westley commented with a smile.

She made a scoffing noise. "Hardly. I was gangly, self-conscious and an easy target."

His eyebrows pinched together. "You were bullied?"

"A little." She didn't like thinking about the laughter of her schoolmates when she'd trip on her way to her desk. Or dropped the beaker full of vinegar in science class. Or when she got so excited during choir because she'd finally hit the right note only to knock three people off the risers, causing bruises and hurt feelings.

She zipped her bag with more force than necessary. "I was mostly uncoordinated. Clumsy. My mother was forever lamenting to anyone who would listen that she didn't dare put out any fragile or breakable keepsakes because the 'little whirlwind' would destroy them."

"You've grown out of that phase," he said as he came up behind her. "Yes, you're enthusiastic, but it's part of your charm. Not to mention you're beautiful, smart and brave."

His words burrowed deep into her soul, soothing the sore spots she long thought healed. Her mouth went dry. She sent up a plea to God above that this was real. That Westley truly saw her how he claimed to.

He moved closer to her, his warm breath ruffling her hair. So close every cell in her body reacted, drawn toward him as if he exuded some magnetic force. She turned slowly to stare up into his handsome face, the memory of his kiss so fresh in her mind.

"You're very distracting," he said as he stepped back slightly.

"You say that like it's a bad thing."

"It has been. We work together. You know the airforce policy on fraternization."

"I'm not under your command."

"Not now, but you will be again." He headed to the door. "We shouldn't linger here."

She knew he was right, of course. Once the threat to her was neutralized, she and Westley would resume their roles at the training center. Which was what she wanted. Right?

"Let me just grab my bagful of lenses." She headed to the closet and went up on tiptoe to reach the box where she kept an assortment of different types of lenses for her camera. Her fingertips clutched the edge and she worked to slide the box from the shelf.

"Here, let me help you." Reaching over her head, Westley grabbed the sides of the box just as she backed up to make room for him. She stepped on his foot, stumbling against him. Reflexively, she fought for balance. Her elbow connected with his midsection as she tried to keep from falling. And succeeded in unintentionally knocking him off his feet. He landed on his backside while the box flew from his hands, the lid flying off and spilling the contents onto the carpet.

Mortified, her face flamed to what she was sure was a bright shade of red. "I'm so sorry."

He stared at her with surprise on his handsome face then he burst into laughter. The deep sound resonated within her chest, eliciting a giggle. Thankfully he wasn't angry at her clumsiness.

The release of hilarity at the situation freed some of her tension. She enjoyed the sound of his laugh and for a moment they were insulated from the dangers of the outside world.

She dropped to her knees beside him to collect her lenses and stared at the small electronic tablet.

She stilled. Her good humor faded, was replaced with a mix of anticipation and dread.

Her gaze lifted to meet Westley's. "I think we've found what the intruder was looking for."

TEN

Westley's laughter died as Felicity's words reverberated through his brain.

I think we've found what the intruder was looking for.

He sat straighter. His ribs were sore from where her boney elbow had made contact, reminding him of his tumble and that for a few minutes he'd let down his guard and enjoyed the moment. He seemed to let loose a lot around Felicity. There was something about her that freed him in ways he hadn't experienced before. Best not to read too much into it, he decided. Instead he focused on her words. "What did you find?"

Felicity pushed aside a lens lying on the carpet to reveal a black tablet the size of a small notebook. "That is not mine."

That piqued his interest. He studied it. "You think your father put it there?"

"I don't know how else it would have gotten into my lens box." She flicked a finger at the device. "This has to contain the evidence that will lead us to my father's killer. This is most likely what the intruder was searching for. He must have only done a cursory look inside this box and since the tablet was at the bottom he missed it."

The same intruder who'd shot Dakota. Thankfully the dog's wound had been superficial, and he was now resting in his kennel. Westley rubbed his chin, contemplating their next move. Should he call the OSI? The crime-scene techs? So far the perpetrator had left no prints, only his DNA through the blood left after Westley wounded him. "We need to see what's on the device before we alert Agent Steffen. Let's take it to the training center and look at it there. I'm not comfortable lingering here."

They collected her lenses and bags then headed out the door. The small hairs at his nape quivered with a sense of foreboding. He glanced around, assessing the area for a threat as he ushered Felicity to the vehicle. Were they being watched?

He couldn't see anyone, but that didn't mean he wasn't out there. Boyd Sullivan, aka the Red Rose Killer, had targeted Felicity. Westley doubted the man would give up easily. Yet, Sullivan wasn't the immediate threat. Whoever killed Felicity's father had also tried to harm Felicity by poisoning her. All in an attempt to keep her from finding the tablet?

When they arrived at the training center, Westley put Felicity's things into the small room they used for the overnight-shift staff. He made a mental note to look at the schedule to coordinate the sleeping arrangements. This wasn't ideal, but would have to do. Keeping Felicity safe meant making the best of the situation.

"I need to check in with Captain Blackwood," he told her.

"I'm going to check on Dakota," Felicity said. "Don't look at the tablet until I can join you."

"I wouldn't dream of it," he assured her. He watched her walk away, feeling like she'd taken the sun with her. He nearly laughed out loud. When had he become poetic?

Disliking having her out of his sight, he followed her to the kennels. He greeted the trainers, who were busy taking care of the dogs. Felicity had kneeled down beside Dakota's crate and was petting him through the metal rungs. The dog licked her hand.

"I gave him his pain meds," a rookie trainer, Lila Fields, told them. "He was whimpering."

"Thank you," Westley said. He liked the single mom. She was competent and compassionate, and very interested in working with dogs suffering from PTSD, though she'd made it clear she didn't want to discuss why she had the special interest.

Felicity glanced up at him with surprise in her eyes. "I thought you were calling the captain."

"I will, but I wanted to see Dakota, too."

She searched his face as if trying to decide if he was telling her the truth. He arched an eyebrow. He did want to make sure the dog was resting but that wasn't his only motivation. But he certainly wasn't going to cop to needing to keep her within arm's length, even though they were safe within the confines of the training center.

A slow smile teased the edges of her mouth and a twinkle appeared in her eyes. She went back to talking to the dog. Did she suspect his true reason for following her? And if so, what did she think? Judging by the smile, she wasn't displeased. His heart rate kicked up a notch. For the millionth time he admonished himself for his base reaction. *Now is not the time.*

Then again, he could be completely wrong about what she was thinking. She wasn't as easy to read as he apparently was.

After a few minutes, Felicity rose and they went to Westley's office and switched on the tablet.

It wasn't password-protected. "That's weird," Felicity said. "Why wouldn't he use a pass code?"

Westley pressed the button for the home screen. There were no apps or email icons, only several folders. All untitled.

"That's so not like my dad. He's usually so organized. You know, 'a place for everything and everything in its place.'"

"Let's have a look at file number one." He clicked on the icon. An album of photos spread across the small screen.

Felicity gasped. "These pictures are from my parents' wedding." She touched the screen, her finger hovering over her parents' images. Her mother looked so pretty in her white wedding gown, her hair piled upon her head and surrounded by a pearl-trimmed veil. Her dad looked handsome in his mess-dress uniform. "I'd only seen the portrait of my parents' wedding day that used to hang in the living room."

"Your parents look happy," Westley said.

They did. Both were smiling. Dad's arm was wrapped around her mother's waist while she held a bouquet of white gardenias. Her mother's favorite flower.

Felicity double-tapped the photo so that it took up the whole screen. As she peered closely at the image staring back at her, a knot formed in the pit of her stomach. Her mother had a distinct bump in her belly. "She was pregnant with me."

Westley tilted his head. "How can you be sure?"

"Look. Can't you see it?" She paced away from his desk, the confines of the office suddenly closing in on her. "This explains so many things." Like why her mother was always hypercritical. And the lectures about making good choices and the consequences of poor choices. "My mind is blowing up."

"Let's not be overdramatic."

"Overdramatic?" She stared at him. "Are you kidding me?" She made a slashing gesture with her hand. "You don't get it. My whole life my mom told me to wait for love. To not get serious about a guy too soon. That every decision I made needed to be well thought out. Not something done in haste or in the heat of the moment." She shook her head at the irony. "Now I understand. Makes total sense. She acted in the heat of the moment and regretted it. Regretted me. No wonder I can never get her approval. She didn't want me to begin with."

Westley came to her side and took her hands. "Look at me," he said. "You can't think that."

"But it's obvious, isn't it?" She felt like the world was crumbling under her feet. "They had to get married. My dad was an honorable man. Of course he married her."

"They had to have loved each other," Westley insisted. "They wouldn't have stayed together for as long as they did if they hadn't loved each other on some level."

"Maybe. But they eventually did divorce." She wanted

to believe him. She wanted to believe that her parents had loved each other. Doesn't every child want that?

She didn't question her father's love. He had made it clear every day of his life. But her mother... All the doubts and fears that she had as a child rose to the surface. She'd tried so hard to make her mother happy and proud. But she'd been doomed from the get-go. "I was a mistake." Numbness stole over her heart.

"Don't say that. Don't let this define you or define your relationship with your mother."

She met his gaze. "But how can I not?"

Determination lit the depths of his eyes. "You can talk to her," he suggested, his tone gentle.

"Like that's going to happen." Just the thought of asking her mother such intimate questions about her life and her marriage made Felicity's insides clench. "You don't know my mother. She can be intimidating at the best of times. I shudder to think how she would react if I asked her if she regretted having me or if she regretted marrying my father. We don't talk about things like that."

Westley drew her to his chest, wrapping his arms around her. "You're right—I don't know her. But she can't be all that bad, because I like her daughter a lot."

He liked her? A lot? The admission surprised her, pleased her. Stirred up all the emotions she'd been trying to ignore. She liked him a lot, too. More than liked him, if she was being honest with herself.

But where could their relationship go? Their future in the air force depended on not becoming involved. There were lines they shouldn't—couldn't—cross.

As much as she wanted to see where this attraction would lead, she knew the best thing for them both was to deny the connection they both obviously felt for one another.

They had a purpose that needed their attention.

She stepped back, took a deep breath. "Let's look at the other files." She wanted to forget what she'd learned, but doubted that knowledge would ever go away. For now she stuffed it into a box within her and hoped the lid would stay shut. "One of the other files has to be related to the case my father was working on."

On the tablet, Westley closed the open file of wedding photos, and then clicked on the next file. More photos appeared. These were of Felicity as a child, and shots of her father and her uncle mugging for the camera. There were photos of her mother as well, looking beautiful and serene sitting on the sand beneath an umbrella. Felicity vaguely remembered going to a Corpus Christi beach. She still had a collection of seashells in her room from that trip. Her mother did look happy here in these photos, she noted.

"These aren't helpful," she said. "Try that one."

Westley exited the file and clicked on the next one. A window popped up and asked for a password. "This has to be it," he said. "Any idea what your father would use as a password?"

"I haven't a clue," she said.

"I'll try your name."

No go.

"Try Colleen," Felicity said. "My mom's name."

That didn't work, either, and neither did the other obvious passwords they tried. He closed the folder and powered down the device before handing it to her. "Hopefully Cyberintelligence can crack the code."

"We have to take this to Ian in the morning," she said. She tucked the device in the deep pocket of her uniform pants. "This may be the evidence he needs to open an official investigation into my dad's death."

Westley's gaze narrowed. "I hope we're not making a mistake by trusting the man."

"We're not." At least she prayed they weren't. But could she trust her judgment? After learning the circumstances behind her parents' marriage, she found herself doubting everything.

Everything? she asked herself. Even her growing feelings for Westley?

The rising sun shone bright over the Texas Hill Country, washing Canyon Air Force Base in shades of gold. Felicity loved this time of day. The world seemed fresh and alive, though she felt a bit wilted from lack of rest. Taking turns on the cot in the training center hadn't provided her much sleep. She feared Westley hadn't received much shut-eye, either.

Only Dakota seemed to have much energy this morning. If his hindquarter wasn't sporting a bandage, she wouldn't have known by his even gait and wagging tail that the dog had been recently hurt.

As Westley drove them back to the OSI offices, with Dakota in the back seat, Felicity glanced out the passenger window at the horizon and sent up a prayer. She had much to pray for. Strength, both physical and mental. Closure for her father's death. Boyd's capture. An untangling of her confusing emotions for Westley.

She told herself she had to be patient. The promise of Romans 8:28 came to mind.

And we know that all things work together for good to them that love God, to them who are the called according to his purpose.

She had to trust that God knew what was needed and He would provide as He saw fit. She filled her lungs with a deep, settling breath. She might not have had the rest she needed, but she felt renewed.

They arrived at the building and rushed inside to Ian's office, but he wasn't there. They backtracked to the front desk.

"Agent Steffen is off base following a lead on the Red Rose Killer case," the woman at the desk told them.

"Can you tell him to contact one of us as soon as possible?" Felicity tried to hide her disappointment. She was anxious to see what was in the password-protected file.

The electronic tablet burned a metaphorical hole in the pocket of her uniform pants. But she couldn't do anything with it until Ian's return. Meanwhile they needed a distraction. "The BMT graduation is this afternoon. I'd like to get some photos of the setup."

With Dakota at their heels, they went to the photo lab, where she picked up her camera. On the way out they ran in to Yvette Crenville. The base nutritionist paused to salute. There were dark circles beneath her eyes, and she looked like she'd lost weight.

"Are you okay?" Felicity asked, worried for the younger woman. They were both targets of Boyd Sullivan. In fact, Felicity figured Boyd would have more reason to feel slighted by Yvette since the woman had made their breakup very public.

Yvette patted her utility cap as if checking to be sure

she'd put it on: "I've been so stressed. This whole thing with Boyd is too much."

"You'd feel better if you had a protection detail," Westley stated.

Felicity certainly did.

Yvette rolled her eyes. "Please. I go to the hospital and my apartment. If I'm not safe at either of those two places, then there is nowhere on base that I'd be safe."

"Having a dog and a handler with you, getting there and back, will give you peace of mind," Felicity told her.

Yvette eyed Dakota and his bandaged hip. "What will give me peace of mind is Boyd back in jail." She adjusted her uniform jacket. "I've been called in to talk to Captain Blackwood again. Like I would help Boyd?" She huffed. "As if. If you ask me, it's Zoe Sullivan they should be questioning. Gotta go." She hurried past them.

Felicity watched Yvette disappear inside the command building. "Do you think she's right? Zoe does seem the most likely to be Boyd's accomplice."

Westley shrugged. "If she is, Linc will find out."

They spent the rest of the day in and around the BMT graduation events. The crush of people made Felicity nervous at first, but with Westley and Dakota watching her six, she relaxed into the process and enjoyed herself, capturing the day's memories. This photography gig wasn't half bad. In fact, she could see herself doing this long-term. Which she would be doing until Boyd was caught.

As dusk settled over the base they returned to where they'd parked the SUV at the back of the lot near the north woods.

She stopped and gripped his arm as dread made her skin prickle.

"Boyd was here." She pointed a shaky finger to the front windshield.

A red rose was tucked under one of the wipers. A small square piece of paper was plastered to the glass.

Westley plucked the note from the windshield, careful to only touch the edge.

"Let me see," she said.

Together they stared at the words typed across the paper.

I'll get you yet.

Her stomach lurched. Boyd was on base. And close.

Anger twisted in Westley's gut. He scanned the area for the fiend, but with so many people milling about, there was no way to tell if Boyd was out there among them.

"I feel so exposed here," she whispered.

He did, too. Despite the fact that they were on a military installation on high alert, somehow Boyd Sullivan managed to move around at will. They could even be in his crosshairs right now. "Don't touch anything. I'll call the captain from the center I need to bag this evidence. Then we're out of here."

From the back compartment of the SUV where he kept supplies, he grabbed a brown paper bag and a set of latex gloves. With the gloves on, he slid the rose and note inside the bag. He placed the offending evidence in the glove box, then opened the doors to let Felicity and Dakota into the SUV. As she passed him to climb in, he touched her arm. "I'm not going to let him, or anyone else, hurt you. Not on my watch."

The look of trust and tenderness in her eyes sent his pulse racing. "I know."

He couldn't stop himself from leaning in and placing a quick kiss on her sweet lips. Her quick inhalation nearly made him steal another, but not now. If ever.

When he closed her door, he shook his head, marveling at the way life was spinning in a direction he'd never expected. From the moment he'd learned that Felicity was in danger, his world had changed. No longer was the future clear. No longer did he know with crystal clarity what he wanted and didn't want in life. He'd thought he had it all mapped out. He'd work at the training center until they forced him to retire. Then he'd open his own dog-training facility. But now he couldn't envision the path before him. Not without Felicity.

He told himself there was only one thing he needed to concentrate on—keeping Felicity safe.

Keeping an alert eye out for any threat, he climbed into the vehicle. He put the key in the ignition, then hesitated. "Why would Boyd leave a note and rose now?"

"Because he's sick?"

"Are we sure Boyd placed them there?" An itch he couldn't name niggled at him. "What if the intruder placed those there to throw us off?"

"To make us think Boyd was the one who poisoned me and broke into my house?" she said. "But we know it wasn't Boyd. It was whoever killed my father." She patted the tablet. "The person is after this."

"Right." His mind whirred with possibilities. Why would the intruder use the note and rose to scare them? Or had Boyd really set them on the hood of Westley's vehicle?

"Don't you think it odd that this note was typed while the first one was handwritten?" Felicity asked.

"It does seem strange." Westley's unease intensified. "Though if you think about it, for the first note he probably didn't have access to a computer and printer."

"True. And whoever is sheltering him has both. I still can't believe anyone on base would help the likes of Boyd."

"People do strange things." Vicious things. Deadly things.

"That's true." She sighed. "Only God knows what really goes on in someone's heart."

Apprehension slithered across his shoulders. He gazed out the front windshield, staring at the dark woods. If Boyd wanted to shoot them he had perfect cover within the trees, yet they sat here unharmed. "We need to get out of the vehicle now."

He didn't wait for her response but hopped out and quickly came around to her side to open her door.

She climbed out. "You think he booby-trapped the car?"

He released Dakota. "I'm not taking any chances."

The dog circled the SUV then dropped to his belly near the front end, his nose aimed toward the undercarriage. A menacing growl filled the air.

"What's he doing?" Felicity asked.

"He sees or smells something that has his hackles up," Westley replied. "That's not his normal alert signal."

Waving Felicity back a safe distance, Westley crawled beneath the vehicle to look for signs of sabotage. A pack of C-4 had been strapped to the undercarriage. There'd been no attempt made to hide either the explosive or the remote detonator blinking a red warning light. Westley froze. Fear like he'd never experienced before blasted through his body.

Felicity's cell phone rang, sending him scrambling out from under the SUV. The look of horror on her pale face matched the sickening dread filling his veins.

She held the phone from her ear. "He says he'll blow up the car if we don't hand over the tablet."

ELEVEN

Felicity's heart stuttered within her chest. Her feet rooted to the spot, she was too afraid to move, afraid if she and Westley and Dakota ran, the man on the phone would detonate the bomb. Westley stepped to her side and took the phone from her hands.

"Who is this?" he demanded. He listened for a moment, his gaze scanning the tree line. "What makes you think we haven't made a copy?"

Still holding the phone in one hand to his ear, Westley grabbed the back of her uniform jacket and pulled her farther away from the vehicle. He let out a shrill whistle and Dakota came running. "Not going to happen, man."

He closed the phone, then yelled, *"Run."*

Galvanized into action by the flood of adrenaline released at his command, Felicity whirled away from the vehicle and ran as fast as her legs could go.

"Get back!" she yelled to the other people going to their nearby cars. "Bomb!"

People scattered, fleeing the area.

When she and Westley, with Dakota at their heels, were a safe distance away, Westley called Security

Forces, alerting them to the bomb strapped to the undercarriage of the SUV.

"What did the man say to you?" Felicity asked after he hung up with the Security Forces dispatcher. She glanced nervously over her shoulder at the SUV, expecting it to explode at any moment.

Westley shook his head. "Nothing for you to worry about."

She gripped his arm in frustration. "Don't do that." She wasn't going to take being coddled.

With a wry twist of his lips, Westley said, "Sorry. He claimed he could get to you at any time and if we didn't leave the tablet and all copies of its contents in your mailbox—without overwatch—tonight, he'd kill you."

A shiver of apprehension wormed its way over her flesh. She was thankful she had two earthly protectors and God watching out for her. And equally grateful Westley told her.

Within minutes the area was evacuated and the bomb squad arrived along with the base's ace bomb-sniffing bloodhound, Annie, and her handler, First Lieutenant Nick Donovan. Felicity and Westley saluted the lieutenant.

Two explosive-ordinance-disposal techs, wearing bombs suits to protect them from the potential blast, approached the vehicle.

Felicity put her hand to her throat, fingering the cross on her necklace, and held her breath.

Within a matter of minutes the EODs had the bomb deactivated and disassembled.

"A crude design," Nick told them. "Amateurish."

"That was a lot of C-4," Westley said.

Nick shrugged. "I'm not saying it wouldn't have fulfilled its purpose."

Which was to kill her and Westley and destroy the evidence in her pocket. She shivered with a ripple of anxiety.

"As a precaution," Nick said, "Annie and I will take a tour of the lot."

"Good idea, Lieutenant," Westley said.

As the explosives expert and his canine walked away, Captain Justin Blackwood arrived. Westley updated him.

"What can you tell me about the caller?" Justin asked.

"Not much," Felicity said. "He sounded muffled, like he had something over the phone." Something niggled at her mind, clamoring for her attention. She tried to hold onto it but whatever her subconscious was trying to say remained elusive. "Maybe the voice sounded vaguely familiar."

"It could have been Sullivan or his accomplice," Justin said. "You may know his accomplice."

"We may *all* know his accomplice," Westley said. "But I'm not convinced this was Sullivan."

Justin peered at him speculatively. "But he left a rose and note on the hood of your vehicle. If it wasn't Boyd or his accomplice, then who?"

Felicity met Westley's gaze. There was no mistaking the question in his eyes. Did they tell the captain about her father's murder?

She nodded. This latest attempt on her life could have ended so badly, not just for her, Westley and Dakota, but also for a multitude of innocent people. They needed to voice their suspicion before it was too late.

"We have something to tell you," Westley said. "But not here."

"I'll drive you back to the training center," Justin said. "You can explain on the way."

They hopped into Justin's vehicle. Dakota nudged his way next to the captain's canine partner, a Belgian Malinois named Quinn. Felicity sat in the back, Westley in front. She sat forward, putting her hand on Westley's shoulder. "Let me explain."

Westley nodded.

"We believe my father was murdered," Felicity informed the captain as he drove. She told him everything Ian had told her and all they knew so far.

Justin glanced sharply at her in his rearview mirror. "So the break-in and the poisoning—those weren't Boyd?"

"No, I—we—believe the man responsible for my father's death was looking for the evidence my father collected during the investigation he was conducting at the time of his death."

"We found an electronic tablet hidden in Felicity's bedroom," Westley told him. "It's what the bomb perp is after."

Not the key they'd found in the desk, just as Ian had predicted.

"How did he know we have it?" Felicity asked. "We haven't told anyone, not even Ian."

"He had to have bugged your house," Justin said.

"We need to do an electronic sweep of the place," Westley said.

"Don't we have an electronics-sniffing dog?" Justin asked.

"We do. She's in training." Felicity couldn't keep

the excitement from her voice. "Senior Airman Chase McLear and Queenie, the cutest little beagle ever, have been in training only a couple months in this new specialty, electronic detection."

"I'll talk to Chase," Westley said.

Justin nodded. "Report back to me tomorrow," he ordered when he pulled over at the training center.

"We will, sir," Westley said as he opened the door. He let Dakota out of the back seat, while Felicity stepped out of the car.

Westley held open the training-center door for Felicity to enter. "You must be exhausted," he said. The warmth in his tone soothed her more than her favorite chocolate melting on the back of her tongue.

"It's been a trying day," she said. "But you must be just as tired."

"I won't lie, I didn't get much sleep," he told her.

"Then I should bite the bullet and ask my uncle if I can stay with him, or rather, if we can stay with him," she said.

He brushed back her hair from her face. "I have the feeling that will be hard for you."

She shrugged. "I don't like asking for help. But I have to get over myself."

He smiled and his approval warmed her heart.

"That's my girl."

His words thrilled her. Was that how he saw her? His girl? She arched an eyebrow. "Girl?"

He made a face. "Please don't take offense."

"I'm teasing you," she said with a grin. "I don't mind being your girl."

Westley's eyes widened and a slow smile spread across his face. "Duly noted."

Heat infused her cheeks. A niggling little voice reminded her that even though he wasn't currently her superior, one day they would go back to the training center and resume their positions within the working-dog program, which meant this thing between them had nowhere to go. Even knowing that, she couldn't muster up regret for the flirty words.

"Let's see if we can find Chase and Queenie," Westley said. "If they have time now, let's go over to the house."

They found Chase, a tall, gentle giant of a man, and his comparatively small beagle in the center of the training ring working with the specialized trainer, Special Agent Denise Logan, on loan from the FBI K-9 Unit. Agent Logan had helped successfully train the FBI's electronics sniffer dogs.

Westley explained what they needed.

"We're game," Chase said, his gaze going to Denise.

The stocky brunette considered the idea as she twisted her wedding ring. "All right. Let's see what Queenie can sniff out. But don't get your hopes up too high. We haven't attempted a listening device."

Felicity sent up a prayer that Queenie and Chase would come through for them. She didn't like the idea that someone had been listening to her every word. The invasion of privacy was somehow worse than having her home ransacked.

Accompanied by Dakota, Westley and Felicity led the way to her house. They went by foot because the evening air had cooled off and she only lived a few blocks away. As they approached, the door of the adjacent house opened and reporter Heidi Jenks stepped out. She waved and hurried down the walkway.

Westley groaned.

"It's fine," Felicity told him and quickened her pace to head off Heidi.

"What's going on?" Heidi asked. She obviously was in for the evening because she had on yoga pants and a T-shirt. But her sharp-eyed gaze took everything in.

"Out for a stroll," Felicity said, skirting the truth. Westley hustled Chase, Denise and the dogs past at a fast clip.

"Looks like something serious is going on," Heidi countered.

"Nothing worth mentioning," Felicity assured her, hoping she'd take the hint.

Heidi pressed her lips together. "I thought we were friends."

Felicity's heart sank. She didn't want to hurt Heidi's feelings. "We are. It's just some things are not for public consumption."

"Not you, too." Heidi huffed. "I did not post the blog."

It took a second for Felicity to connect what Heidi meant, then she remembered that an anonymous blogger had leaked the information about Zoe Sullivan visiting her half brother, Boyd, in prison. "I know you didn't." At least Felicity hoped not.

Westley caught her attention with a wave from the porch of her house, where he and Dakota kept watch. Her heart did a little jig in her chest. She had to admit she didn't mind having the two males worry over her.

"Look, I've got to go." She strode away, aware of Heidi's gaze.

When she reached the porch, Westley slipped his hand around her elbow. "Was she fishing for information?"

Wanting to protect her friend, she said, "She's curious. Wouldn't you be if you saw all of us coming down the street?"

"I don't know if I trust her," Westley said. "She could be Boyd's accomplice for all we know."

"I highly doubt it," Felicity said. "Heidi may be ambitious, but she's not corrupt."

He lifted a shoulder. "You never know."

She didn't like the doubt he'd planted in her mind. She glanced across the side yard separating the two houses. Heidi remained on her porch watching them, but Felicity refused to believe ill of her neighbor.

Wanting to redirect their focus, Felicity said, "Let's see how Chase and Queenie are doing."

Inside the house, Denise put her finger to her lips, indicating they were to remain silent while Chase and Queenie worked. As the dog sniffed around the couch and coffee table, Westley and Felicity stood back with Dakota sitting in front of them, his dark eyes watching the other dog.

Queenie sat by the end table, her tail wagging. Chase gave the dog a treat, then kneeled down and felt the underside of the small table. He smiled and peeled away a small, round device and held it up.

Felicity couldn't believe it. She had actually been bugged. Westley's grim expression told her he'd expected as much.

Denise took the device and inspected it, then nodded before placing the electronic bug into an evidence bag. Then she made a motion for the pair to continue on.

They all followed as the beagle led them down the hallway to Felicity's bedroom.

Felicity winced as the pair entered the room. She

and Westley and Denise filled the doorway to watch Queenie sniff the bed and the floor around the closet, then finally come to a halt at the dresser. Chase opened the bottom drawer. Queenie sniffed but didn't alert. Two more drawers were opened before the beagle alerted. Inside the top drawer was a listening device. It was the same drawer that had been open the morning Felicity had awoken to find someone at the foot of her bed. She shuddered with revulsion. The intruder had been spying on her. That was how he known about the tablet. But did he know about the key? Was the key even significant?

Chase and Queenie checked the rest of the house and found no more devices.

Denise took the evidence bags and set them outside before coming back into the house. "I'll have those sent to the FBI lab for analysis." Then she turned to Chase. "This was a successful test," she said, obviously pleased. "I'm proud of you both."

Despite the sick roil in her belly from having been bugged, a smile tugged at the corner of Felicity's mouth at the sight of the red creeping up Chase's neck at the compliment. She slanted a glance at Westley. He raised an eyebrow at her. She wanted to poke at him about how easy it was to give praise, but decided she didn't need to point out the obvious.

"Good job," Westley told Chase. Felicity couldn't stop the grin this time. And she hadn't had to say a word. Okay, maybe she'd given him a look but still... he could learn. That warmed her heart.

Chase shrugged. "It wasn't me. Queenie did all the sniffing."

Westley clapped the other man on the back. "We appreciate it just the same."

Looking decidedly uncomfortable, Chase tugged at the collar of his uniform. "We'll head back to the training center now if you don't need us anymore."

"No, you're good," Westley said.

Chase, Queenie and Denise left the house, taking the devices with them.

"Now what?" Felicity said. "Do you think it's safe to come back here?"

"Not yet," he said. "I want to install a security system before you do. Tonight we'll bunk with your uncle and then tomorrow I'll make this house a fortress."

She appreciated all he was doing for her. "Thank you. I don't know if I could handle all of this without you."

A frown formed on his handsome face. "You're strong, Felicity. I have no doubt you can handle anything life throws at you."

His words sent pleasure sliding through her. She had the strongest urge to kiss him, but considering they were standing on her porch beneath the light, where anyone could see them, she refrained. Instead, she focused on the job they still had to do. "We need to get the tablet to Ian before anything else happens."

"You're right," Westley said. "Why don't you call and see if he's back on base?"

"Can do." Felicity fished out her cell phone from the pocket of her uniform pants and dialed the OSI office. On the third ring, the receptionist answered.

"He's in a meeting with Lieutenant General Hall and Captain Blackwood," the woman said when Felicity asked for Ian. "I'm sure he'll contact you when he's done. I gave him your earlier message."

Felicity thanked the woman and hung up. She related the information to Westley. "I hope this means there's been a break in the Red Rose Killer case. We'll all sleep better once Boyd is back behind bars."

"This is true," Westley agreed. "But I won't sleep at all until the maniac who killed your father is captured." He curled his fingers around her hand that held the tablet. "We need to get this to a secure place until we can pass it off to Agent Steffen."

"It would be safe with you," she said, willing to let him carry the burden.

"I have an idea," he said. "There's a small safe in the office of the training center, where we keep the paperwork on the dogs and an emergency stash of their medication. The tablet will be safe there tonight."

"Good idea." She held his gaze. The tender expression on his handsome face made her pulse jump.

She knew she could count on him to protect her and find a solution to any problem. He was a man of honor and integrity. A man worthy of loving.

Her mouth went dry at that thought. Was she falling in love with Westley?

She had to admit that maybe she was.

It was such a strange sensation, considering not that long ago she wasn't sure she liked him or that he liked her. But things had changed between them at a rapid clip.

A pang tugged at her heart. She didn't see a way for them to ever be a couple. Not if they hoped to continue to train the dogs, with her under his command.

Best to put any thoughts of romance out of her mind and close off her heart before they both got hurt.

* * *

Felicity stepped back, putting space between her and Westley. He could sense her withdrawing from him emotionally. He wasn't sure what thought had crossed her mind to make the small *V* appear between her eyebrows. For a moment there, as they stood beneath the glow of the porch light, he'd seen the spark of attraction that seemed to simmer within her and flared occasionally when he least expected it. He savored those moments. Even though he knew there could never be anything real or long-lasting between them. Still, it was nice to pretend for a second here and there…

"I should call my uncle," she said, her voice tight. "See if we can stay there tonight."

"Right." It was the right call. Her uncle was family. They would both be more comfortable there than taking shifts on the cot. "Let's go to the training center and take care of the tablet, then you can call him."

They walked back, Dakota trotting beside them. Westley wanted to ask her if she was okay, but that seemed like a dumb question considering all that had transpired. Of course she wasn't all right. She had to be stressed and scared, and was putting up a brave front. No, not a front. She was brave. And kind and so much stronger in spirit than he'd given her credit for in the beginning.

He admired and respected Felicity. Enough to know that he had to keep his emotions in check so as not to ruin her career or her life.

At the training center, they tucked the tablet into the small safe located in the desk cabinet. Then Felicity called her uncle.

"Thanks, Uncle Patrick, we'll see you soon," she said

as she hung up. Then she looked up at Westley. "He's happy to be of help."

"I hope he won't mind Dakota staying with us," Westley said.

Felicity pulled a face. "Uncle Patrick isn't fond of dogs."

"So I noticed," Westley said. "But he'll have to deal with it."

Felicity scratched Dakota behind the ears. "Uncle Patrick just has to get to know you. He'll see not all dogs are scary."

She grabbed her bag from the cot room and followed Dakota and Westley outside to the parking lot. Westley had the keys to the vehicle used by Caleb Streeter because Westley's SUV was now in the custody of Security Forces.

They drove to the set of apartments at the north end of the base, where her uncle had a unit on the fifth floor. They took the elevator up and knocked on her Uncle Patrick's door. He opened it immediately. He stood in the open doorway in his socks, regulation sweatpants and a T-shirt stretched over his broad shoulders.

Dakota emitted a low growl. Westley glanced at Dakota. The hair along his back raised in a ridge. His tail was up, his ears stiff. What was that about?

Patrick's gaze bounced from Felicity to Westley and then landed on Dakota. "Oh, no. He's not staying."

"Only way Felicity and I stay is if Dakota does," Westley stated firmly. He wasn't going to trust anyone, not even himself, with Felicity's safety without extra protection.

A deep scowl created lines along Patrick's forehead. "I don't like dogs."

As if he understood the words, Dakota bared his teeth in a snarl and lunged at Patrick, sending him stumbling backward with horror on his face.

TWELVE

"Dakota, no!" Felicity's heart slammed against her chest. What was going on? She'd never seen the dog go into attack mode without provocation. The only times she'd witnessed Dakota's true fierceness was in demonstrations where Westley or one of the other trainers wore a padded bite suit. She hurried across the room to stand in front of her uncle. She held a hand to Dakota. "Stop!"

Westley reeled in Dakota and grabbed his collar, holding back the snapping and snarling dog.

"Stand off! Heel!" Westley commanded in a loud tone that reverberated through the apartment.

Dakota slowly complied and sat, but his intense focus was trained on Patrick. His teeth were still bared but he'd quieted down to a low, ominous growl.

"Put that away!" Westley said, his gaze on something over Felicity's shoulder.

She whirled to find her uncle holding his service weapon in shaky hands. Thankfully the barrel was aimed at the floor.

"Get that beast out of here or I'll shoot it!" Uncle Patrick yelled. Sweat gleamed on his forehead.

"Whoa." Felicity held up both hands, now needing to protect Dakota. "Uncle Patrick, lower the weapon. Westley will take Dakota back to his kennel."

Uncle Patrick didn't seem to hear her. His fear-filled gaze was on Dakota.

Afraid the situation would careen even further out of control, Felicity faced Westley. "Take him back to the center."

"Felicity—" Westley warned, even as he tugged on Dakota's leash, forcing the dog to retreat into the hallway. Felicity hurried to the door. She closed it to a crack, her gaze on Westley. "I'll be fine."

"I shouldn't be leaving you."

"It's okay. I'll be fine. He's my uncle, after all."

"I'll check on you after I get Dakota settled." He shook his head. "I don't get what got him so riled up."

"He must sense Uncle Patrick's animosity toward dogs," she said. Why else would Dakota go into full attack mode?

Westley nodded but he was clearly perplexed and upset by the situation. So was she. They trained for these variables. They couldn't have an unpredictable dog in the program. She only hoped this was an anomaly and not a new pattern of behavior for the German shepherd.

She shut the door and leaned against it. Her pulse galloped along her veins. She took several calming breaths, glad to see her uncle had set the gun on the dining-room table. He crossed to the bar and poured himself a tumbler of amber liquid. He held up the glass. "Want a drink?"

She shook her head. "No. Thank you." She blew out

a breath. "I'm not sure what got into Dakota. He's not like that normally."

"Mongrel beast should be put down," Uncle Patrick growled.

"No!" The thought of Dakota being euthanized because he'd thought he'd been protecting her nearly made her knees buckle.

Patrick downed his drink in one long swallow then poured himself another and moved to sit on the couch. "I hate dogs."

Trying to understand the virulence in Patrick's voice, she moved to sit across from him. "Mom told me you had a horrible experience with a dog once. What happened?"

Patrick leaned his head back against the couch and stared off as if remembering. "When we were kids, your mom and I would get off the school bus in the neighborhood before ours because it was quicker to walk home across the Moselys' field than wait a half an hour for the bus to circle around to our house. Mr. Mosely kept the field mowed but that spring he'd died and the field became overgrown. Still, we made a path through the tall grass and weeds." He sipped from his drink.

"One day a large mutt charged through the grass, barking and snarling." He shuddered and took another drink. "He belonged to Mr. Mosely's adult son."

"How old were you?"

He glanced at her. "Ten. Your mom was eight. She was a couple feet ahead of me on the path. I yelled for her to run but she froze." He rubbed a hand over his jaw. "I still can see her standing there. The look of terror on her face. That dog closing in on her. I reacted. I pushed her out of the way in the nick of time." He lifted his pant leg to reveal his calf muscle. "They're faint now, but I carry the scars of that dog's teeth."

She winced. No wonder her uncle had freaked out at Dakota's behavior. Felicity's heart hurt for her uncle and her mother. She could imagine the horror the two children experienced. "You saved Mom. You were a hero."

Patrick snorted. "Yeah. That's what everyone said. It didn't make the pain or the fear or the nightmares go away."

She could relate to lingering fear and nightmares. "I'm sorry. If I had known, we wouldn't have brought Dakota over."

He swirled the last of his drink before gulping it down. "Just keep the beast away from me."

"I will." She stood and picked up her bags by the front door. She needed to freshen up and have a moment alone. "Where shall I put my things?"

He waved toward a short hallway. "You can take the bedroom. On the right. Bath to the left. I'll sleep out here on the couch. And the master sergeant can use a bedroll when he returns."

She carried her bag to the bedroom and sank onto the edge of the bed. Propping her elbows on her knees, she dropped her head into her hands. Life had become a roller coaster. She was ready to jump off and be on even ground.

Her cell phone rang. She fished it from her pocket.

"Hey, you okay?" Westley's deep voice filled her head.

Relaxing back on to the bed, she replied, "Yes. Boy, oh, boy. What a day." She told him about the dog attack her uncle had suffered as a child.

"That explains your uncle's reaction, but not Dakota's. I've asked Dr. Roark to take a look at him when he has a free moment to make sure there's nothing medically wrong."

She sat up. "Oh, I hope that's not it." Or maybe she did hope so because then they could treat him. "Is Dakota calm now?"

"Not really. He hasn't been aggressive at all but he can't seem to focus and he keeps pacing back and forth in his kennel. Frankly I'm afraid to leave him until Dr. Roark can take a look at him. He did not want to leave your uncle's apartment complex. I practically had to drag him to the vehicle and then had to pick him up and put him in because he wouldn't jump in himself."

"That's so weird. There's no need for you to return here tonight. Stay with Dakota."

"Are you sure?"

"Yes, I'm safe here."

"Before I forget to tell you, Rusty found Riff and brought him in."

Her heart lifted. "That's good news."

A photo album on the bottom shelf of the bedside table caught her attention. She took it from the shelf and set it on the bed.

"On another note, I have a security company coming tomorrow morning to arm your house. Once they have the system in place you can return home."

"That's good." She flipped open the photo album. She wouldn't have pegged Uncle Patrick as the sentimental type to keep pictures in an album. The first page was of a bald-headed baby lying on a blanket. Uncle Patrick, she assumed. He was a cute baby. "I'm sure Uncle Patrick will be more than happy to have his bedroom back after he spends the night on his lumpy-looking couch."

Westley chuckled. "Couldn't be much worse than the cot at the center."

"Or the barracks," she countered. She flipped through the pages, smiling at the baby pictures of her uncle.

"True. I don't miss those bunks."

She ran a finger over the image of her mother as a baby. "Do you ever think about giving up your studio apartment for a house?"

"Someday."

When he had a wife and family? The thought snuck up on her. She wondered what it would take to make this man settle down. Did she have what it took to be the one he settled down with? Did she want that? A quiver of nerves ran through her as she realized there was a part of her that very much wanted a future with Westley. But how could she and still hope to work with the dogs?

"I should let you get some rest," he said. "I'm staying at the center a little longer. With Dakota behaving the way he is, I think I'd better keep an eye on him until he's less agitated. If you need anything, call me and I'll be right there."

"I will. I promise." She hung up and scooted to the head of the bed to lean against the wall. She continued to look through the photo album. There were many pictures of her uncle and mother as they grew up together. It was fun to see her mother going from a gap-toothed child, to a girl, to a teen, and finally to a young woman. The last few pages of the album held photos similar to the ones on the tablet.

One image held her attention. It was the same picture

of her father and Uncle Patrick that was on the tablet, but in this one, they were sitting on motorcycles. Two black bikes. And both men were dressed in black leather and holding black helmets.

Her hand went to the chain around her neck. Did the key belong to a motorcycle her father had once owned?

She scrambled off the bed, taking the photo album with her. In the kitchen she found Uncle Patrick drinking a beer and eating smoked salmon.

"Are you hungry?" he asked as she entered.

Taking a seat at the counter, she answered, "A little, actually." She laid the photo album open on the granite top. "I didn't know you and Dad rode motorcycles."

Patrick flicked a glance at the album. "Yep. Those were the good old days."

"Whatever happened to my dad's bike?" She'd never seen him on one.

"Colleen didn't like it, so he sold it."

She studied the motorbike in the photo. Remembering Linc's certainty of the type of bike the key on her gold chain fit, she asked, "Was Dad's motorcycle a BMW 2 series?"

Patrick's shoulders visibly stiffened. He slowly turned toward her. "Why would you ask about that specific bike?"

The coldness in his tone sent a chill sliding down her spine. Her mind scrambled to see why her question would upset him. Should she tell him about the key? She couldn't see what harm it would be to show him what she'd found. She tugged the chain out from beneath her uniform top and held up the key. "I found this in Dad's desk."

Patrick took a long swig of his beer and wiped his

mouth with the back of his hand before setting the bottle on the counter and closing the distance between them to stare at the key. He crossed his arms over his barrel chest. "No. Your father rode a Ducati."

"Oh." She wasn't sure what to make of Uncle Patrick's strange reaction to the key. Her gaze strayed back to the picture. The two bikes did look a bit different. She lifted her gaze. "Was your motorcycle the BMW?"

"It was."

Her heart beat a bit faster in her chest. "Where's the bike now?"

"Scrap yard."

"A long time ago, right?" She hoped, because the thought forming in her mind was causing distress to strangle her from the inside out. Uncle Patrick couldn't be the rider of the motorcycle that had struck the pedestrian and left him paralyzed, could he?

"Where's your father's tablet, Felicity?"

Her breath hitched. She strove to keep her cool as panic flared in her gut and lit a hot path to her brain. Oh, no. No, no, no. Uncle Patrick couldn't be her father's murderer. He couldn't be the one who'd tried to poison her. The one who had shot at Westley.

Oh! Lungs tight from lack of air, the world tilted as the realization slid home. Dakota had snapped at the man who'd shot him.

"Where is it?" Patrick demanded again.

Sliding from the stool, Felicity faced her uncle. "You killed my father."

Patrick's eyes narrowed. "He fell off the ladder."

Anger infused her. "Did he? Or did you stage it to look that way?"

Lips thinning, Patrick stepped closer. "Don't mess with me."

Refusing to be intimidated, she stood her ground. "You were the one riding the motorcycle that hit the young man and then rode away."

"He stepped out from between two cars," Patrick said, his words an admission and an excuse.

"Then why didn't you stop and help him?"

"That's exactly what your father asked."

"It's a valid question." Her gaze went to the beer bottle then back to him. "You were drinking."

"I'd had a few. I didn't see the guy. It wasn't my fault. But your father demanded I turn myself in." He let out a bitter laugh. "Like that was going to happen."

"So you killed him?" Her heart bled with grief over the senselessness of it all. If Patrick had just owned up to his crime, her dad would still be alive.

"Graham wouldn't listen." Patrick moved toward her. "I want that tablet, Felicity. And any copies you made."

She narrowed her gaze. Copies? "You're the one who planted the bomb in Westley's vehicle and called me. I knew I recognized the voice." And Dakota had recognized his scent on the explosives.

His face twisted. "I should have just blown you all up."

"Why did you leave the note and rose?" She let out a humorless laugh. "Oh, I know, to pin your crime on the Red Rose Killer."

"I'm still going to pin my crimes on that maniac."

Her stomach knotted at the implication in her uncle's words. "I'm leaving."

He grabbed her arm. "No. You're going to give me that tablet."

"I don't have it." She jerked her arm from him and backed away. Her gaze landed on the dining room table a few feet from her, where her uncle's service weapon still sat. If she could get to it… She edged toward the table.

Patrick lunged forward, knocking her to the side and pouncing on his gun. She regained her balance, but he swung the barrel toward her.

She stilled, her hands up. Her heart plummeted. Fear turned her blood to ice, making her ache with dread. "Don't do anything rash."

"Where's the tablet?" He advanced on her.

"At the training center where all those *beasts* are." She had the satisfaction of seeing her uncle blanch.

She sent up a silent plea to God that somehow, someway, Westley would be able to disarm her uncle before he killed her or anyone else.

"There's nothing medically wrong with this dog," Dr. Roark told Westley. "His wound is healing nicely. His heart rate is normal and so is his temperature."

Motioning for a much calmer Dakota to jump off the exam table, Westley said, "That's good to know but it doesn't explain his strange aggression toward Felicity's uncle."

Dr. Roark pumped hand sanitizer on his palm and rubbed his hands together. "Had he and Dakota ever met?"

Westley thought about that. "Yes." Patrick had shown up at Felicity's house. "But Dakota hadn't reacted at all then."

"Something must have happened between then and

today," the doctor suggested. "Something that made Dakota want to lash out?"

But what? Westley hadn't seen her uncle again until a little while ago. Could it be that Dakota had sensed the other man's fear and reacted? No, Dakota wouldn't have shown such extreme hostility because of the other man's fear.

It was a puzzle that Westley intended to unravel because he couldn't have an undisciplined dog in the program. He would have to do some research and see if there was something in Dakota's background before he came to Canyon that might explain his behavior.

With Dakota by his side, they left the vet clinic and headed along the now darkened street toward the training center. When they reached the edge of the parking lot, Westley stopped short. A thought rammed into him with the force of a missile.

What if Dakota had reacted so violently because he recognized the scent of the man who'd shot him?

The realization made Westley stumble, and nearly go to his knees.

Felicity!

He had to get to her. To warn her. To protect her. From her uncle.

At a run, he led Dakota to one of the training-center vehicles. He had keys to all the SUVs on his keychain. Quickly, he and Dakota jumped inside. He fumbled to find the right key and stuck it into the ignition.

Headlights cut across the parking lot as one of the maintenance trucks pulled in and came to an abrupt halt. The driver's door flew open, and Staff Sergeant Patrick Dooley hopped out, a gun in his hand.

Dakota let out a snarl.

"Quiet," Westley admonished, not wanting to alert the other man to their presence. Breath lodged in his throat, he watched Patrick motion with the gun and Felicity climbed out of the vehicle.

Westley's heart stuttered to a crawl. Patrick was forcing Felicity to turn over the tablet. But what would Patrick do when he realized she didn't have the combination to the safe?

Holding his breath, Westley waited until Felicity and her uncle disappeared into the training center before he and Dakota jumped out of the SUV and raced to the door.

There was no time to call for backup. Westley had to get inside before Patrick did something drastic.

Swallowing back the fear of losing Felicity, Westley felt determination burn through his gut. He would do anything to save the woman he loved.

THIRTEEN

With the barrel of the gun pressing hard against her ribs, Felicity led the way through the training center toward the back office. The muted sound of dogs barking from the kennel filled the hallway.

Glancing at her uncle, she noticed the beads of sweat on his brow and the tightness around his mouth. He was nervous. After hearing of his horrific ordeal when he'd been attacked by a vicious dog, she wanted to feel sorry for him, but any sort of tender emotions toward her uncle were gone.

He'd basically admitted to killing her father, who'd supposedly been his best friend, and trying to kill her, his own niece.

Her mother was going to be devastated.

Felicity's heart hurt for her mom.

As they passed the break room, Lila Fields stepped out, nearly ramming into them.

"Oh, I'm sorry," the rookie trainer said, almost dropping the plate in her hand along with a buttered bagel.

"No problem." Felicity tried to keep her voice neutral and not let the panic show.

Lila's curious gaze landed on Patrick. "Hello."

Felicity gritted her teeth. The last thing she needed was Lila asking questions or becoming suspicious that something was wrong. She didn't want anybody else's life in danger. She needed Lila to go about her business so that Uncle Patrick wouldn't feel the need to harm the woman.

Hoping to keep her voice free of the fear making her heart boom in her ears and her fingertips tingle, she said, "Lila, this is my Uncle Patrick. We're looking for Westley. Is he in his office?"

"No, I believe he took Dakota to the vet."

Felicity's stomach sank. She wasn't sure what to do now. When Uncle Patrick realized she didn't know how to get into the safe, he would go ballistic. She had to figure out a way to overpower him. A dismal prospect. He outweighed her by half, at least.

"We'll wait for him, then," Uncle Patrick said. "In his office."

He gave Felicity a nudge with the barrel of the gun, effectively keeping the weapon out of sight, and kept his fingers tightly around her biceps.

Leaving Lila with a nod, they continued down the hall. Once inside the office, Patrick gave her a little shove, forcing her to the middle of the room, while he shut the door.

"Where's the tablet?"

"It's in the safe." She visually swept the room, searching for something to disarm him with, or to knock him out.

Anger for all he'd done—a hit-and-run, killing her father, trying to kill her—burned like a torch inside of her. But there was nothing within reach to use as a weapon. Frustration beat against her temple. Her fingers curled at her side.

Waving the gun, Patrick said, "Where's the safe?"

Felicity swallowed back the anxiety dampening her anger. "In the desk cabinet to the right."

Uncle Patrick moved to inspect the cabinet. Taking advantage of his distraction, she edged toward the door, hoping to make an escape. If she could get to the kennels, she could let the dogs loose. Uncle Patrick might run away.

Or shoot one of the canines.

On second thought, she couldn't put the animals at risk, either.

"Take one more step and you'll regret it," Uncle Patrick said, aiming the weapon at her head. "Open the safe."

"I don't have the combination." Holding up her hands, she spoke calmly, much more calmly than she felt. "Only Westley does."

She wasn't sure if that was true. She supposed Caleb Streeter had access, but she wouldn't volunteer that information. Who knew what Uncle Patrick would do.

Uncle Patrick plopped down into one of the two side chairs and put his feet up on the desk. "Then we'll wait for Master Sergeant James."

Apprehension bubbled up in her chest. She wished there was a way to warn Westley. She hated the thought of him walking in blind to the situation.

She remained standing where she was between Uncle Patrick and the door, hoping that when Westley came in she could provide a shield. She could only pray that Lila would see Westley before he headed to the office and tell him they were waiting.

At least that would give him a heads-up. But it wouldn't tell him to be cautious. He had no idea her uncle was the one behind her father's murder and the attempts on her life.

She hoped Westley would cooperate with her uncle because she couldn't stand it if anything happened to him.

Deep inside she had to admit her concern for Westley's welfare not only stemmed from the fact that they were friends and worked closely together, but also because her feelings for him had morphed into something that left her breathless.

She loved Westley.

If the circumstances weren't so dire and precarious, she'd sink to the floor with the knowledge that she'd fallen in love with the one man she shouldn't. Not if she hoped to return to the training center under his command.

It was a problem she had no idea how to resolve. She prayed there would be time to figure it out.

Westley kept Dakota at his side as they eased into the back entrance of the training center. The overhead light revealed the hallway was empty. Knowing Felicity's uncle would go nowhere near the dogs, Westley figured they had headed to the office. He needed to get there before anything happened to Felicity. With caution tightening his shoulder muscles, he and Dakota hustled to the office. The door was closed.

Dakota sniffed the edge of the door. The hair on his back raised, alerting to the fact that the dog smelled the enemy. Westley gave Dakota the hand signal used by soldiers for combat silence and then motioned for the dog to take up a position on his belly to the side of the door out of the line of sight.

Feeling the need to ask God for help, Westley sent up a quick prayer. Hope that the Lord above would hear his plea bolstered his resolve. He dug his phone from his pocket and put it on silent, then dialed Captain Blackwood's cell.

Leaving the line open, he tucked the cell into his breast pocket and reached for the door handle. On a deep breath, he swung the door open, careful to keep to the side in case Patrick had a twitchy trigger finger.

Felicity stood in the middle of the room, her surprised gaze meeting his. She mouthed, *He's got a gun.*

Giving her a nod, Westley decided to play ignorant. "What's going on?"

"Come in, Master Sergeant," Patrick drawled from the chair facing the desk. "Put your hands in the air."

Complying, Westley walked through the door and moved to stand next to Felicity. "What's with the gun, Staff Sergeant Dooley?"

Patrick's feet hit the floor. "I want the tablet."

"Okay. I'll give it to you." Obviously the man wasn't thinking clearly. There was no way he'd walk out of here unscathed. They were in a public place. One yell and reinforcements would come. But Westley had questions, and the best way to learn the answers was to appease him. "Tell me why you've been trying to kill your niece."

"It's that serial killer's fault," Patrick said. "He targeted Felicity. I knew once that happened there would be extra scrutiny on her and eventually there'd be questions about Graham's death. Agent Steffen was sniffing around, trying to reopen the investigation. I had to make sure there was nothing left of Graham's investigation to point to me."

"Are you admitting to killing Agent Monroe?" Westley asked him.

"I'm not admitting anything."

"But my father's case notes will convict you of the hit-and-run," Felicity said.

"I told you that was an accident," Patrick said.

"And poisoning Felicity? Was that an accident?"

"It would have worked if that dog hadn't intervened," Patrick groused. "Everyone would have thought that psycho had made good on his threat. And then I could have found the tablet."

Felicity took a step forward. "What did you do with my father's laptop?"

The older man snorted. "It's at the bottom of the Gulf of Mexico." Patrick waved his gun. "Now give me that tablet! Once I destroy the thing, there won't be any evidence."

Afraid that Patrick's agitated state would lead to him shooting Felicity, Westley tucked her behind him, where he could protect her. "Once we give you the evidence, then what? Are you going to kill us, too? Both of us?"

A scowl wrinkled Patrick's forehead. "I'll have to, won't I? Even if you couldn't prove what happened was my fault, you'd make my life miserable. But I'll make sure to blame it on the Red Rose Killer."

The man was definitely unhinged if he thought he'd get away with his scheme. Keeping a hand on Felicity and forcing her to move in tandem with him, Westley edged slowly around to the other side of the desk, leaving a clear path from the doorway to Patrick. "Boyd Sullivan is a convenient scapegoat."

"You won't get away with it," Felicity said. "Agent Steffen will discover your crimes."

"He hasn't yet," Patrick said. "Now, open the safe."

Knowing they had one shot at this, Westley tugged Felicity into a crouch in front of the safe. In a loud, clear voice, Westley yelled, "Get 'em!"

Dakota sprang into action, charging into the room and going straight for Patrick's leg. His powerful jaw latched on. Patrick let out a yowl of pain and terror. Westley jumped up and vaulted over the desk, grabbing the gun and wresting it away from the other man.

Aiming the weapon at Patrick's chest, Westley gave the commands, "Out! Heel!"

The dog immediately let go and backed up to a sit beside Westley. But Dakota's body was tense and poised, ready to attack if given the command.

Patrick crumpled to a heap, his hands holding on to his leg. Felicity grabbed the desk lamp and lifted it high over her uncle's head.

"Felicity, no. It's over," Westley said, afraid she'd follow through on the intent in her eyes. He didn't want her to have that regret. "I have him covered. He's not going anywhere."

Slowly, her gaze cleared and she lowered the lamp, setting it carefully back on the desk. Stiffly, she moved to stand next to Dakota. She put a hand on his head. "Good dog."

The sound of pounding feet filled the room and a moment later several Security Forces officers stormed in with weapons drawn. Then Captain Blackwood stepped inside, followed by Ian.

"It seems you have everything under control, Master Sergeant James," the captain said. Holding up his phone, he added, "We heard everything."

Lowering the gun and handing it to Security Forces, Westley told Felicity, "I dialed the captain's cell before I entered."

She blinked up at him with surprise lighting the depths of her eyes. "How did you know?"

"I realized that Dakota was reacting to the scent of the man who'd shot him when he went into attack mode back at your uncle's apartment," he explained. "I should have figured that out right away. I'm so sorry you had to go through this."

"I didn't see it at first, either," she told him. "He's family." She watched as the Security Forces officers dragged her uncle from the room in handcuffs. Westley put his arm around her shoulders, offering her what comfort he could. It took every ounce of willpower he possessed not to gather her in his arms and hold her close and never let her go.

"I thought I could trust him." She shook her head, sadness pulling at the corners of her mouth. He wanted to kiss away her disappointment and hurt.

"I found a photo of him and my dad on motorcycles," she said. "That's when I realized he was the one whom my dad was investigating for the hit-and-run." She let out a bitter sound. "He said my dad had wanted him to turn himself in, but Uncle Patrick refused. Instead, he killed my father and made it look like an accident."

"You can rest easy now," Ian said.

"No," Westley countered, his heart rate jumping. "She's still a target of the Red Rose Killer."

"Of course," Ian stated. "That's not what I meant at all. We have closure now on Agent Monroe's death. The

family of the hit-and-run victim will appreciate knowing the man who paralyzed their son will be charged
with multiple crimes and spend the rest of his life in
prison."

It was justice. But it would be painful for the Monroe family.

"What is the latest intel on Sullivan?" Westley asked.

"There have been reported sightings all over the
state," Justin answered. "We're not sure of the reliabil-
ity of any of the information. Our best guess is Boyd is
paying people to claim they've seen him."

Westley's gut clenched. She was still in danger. Not
only from the maniac serial killer known as the Red
Rose Killer, but also from Westley's feelings for her.
He didn't know how he could continue to be detailed to
her protection while keeping his love for her a secret.
He wasn't that good at subterfuge.

He was going to have to trust that God would watch
over her and arrange for someone else to be assigned
to her protection detail. For both their sakes.

"You're what?" Felicity stared at Westley. Sunlight
filtering through the blinds of the photo lab gleamed in
his dark hair. His beret was tucked into the pocket of
his battle-ready uniform as he stood with his hands stiff
at his sides, and his strong jaw was set in a determined
line. Beside him Dakota tilted his head, his dark-eyed
gaze bouncing between them.

"You can't asked to be rotated off my detail," she
stated flatly.

Why would he do that? Her pulse pounded with
adrenaline as if she'd run a marathon. Every vital system in her went on alert at hearing such disturbing news.

"It's a good idea if we don't spend as much time together," he said in a rush.

Disbelief washed over her. "You don't want to spend time with me?"

He grimaced. "No. That's not it."

"I'm pretty certain that is what you just said."

"I'm botching this."

She planted her fists on her hips. "You think?" A ribbon of frustration wound around her heart.

Rolling his shoulders, he said, "The training center needs me."

"I thought Caleb was handling things there."

"He is."

"But you're not happy with his work?"

"No. I mean, that's not what I'm saying."

Her head was spinning. She wished he'd be clearer. "Then...?"

"Caleb is doing a great job, but there are just some things that need to be taken care of, that need my attention. And still so many dogs are missing. I need to focus on finding the dogs."

She wasn't quite sure she believed that excuse. Yes, the dogs were a priority. One she could help him with. She really didn't want to take offense at him basically standing here telling her he didn't want to be with her, but she couldn't help the sense of betrayal. Hurt. Disappointment flooded her veins. The training center had been running fine for the past week, and would continue to. But that really wasn't the issue, was it?

She'd thought she and Westley had come so far. She'd thought he felt the same way toward her. She'd hoped he'd fallen in love with her the way she'd fallen in love with him. Apparently, she was wrong.

"You don't want to protect me anymore." The words tasted bitter on the tongue. "Okay, I get it. You didn't want the detail in the first place. I don't even know why you agreed to it."

She walked away from him, stopping at the desk to picked up her camera. She fiddled with the lenses, trying hard not to let the tears burning the back of her eyes fall. Her heart crumbled, the pain sharp.

He came up behind her, awareness seared her clean through. His hands rested lightly on her shoulders and gave her a gentle squeeze.

"Felicity, it's not that I don't want to protect you. I do, but I can't."

She didn't understand. He wasn't making sense. He'd done a wonderful job so far. He and Dakota.

She turned around and stared into Westley's handsome face. There was distress in his eyes.

Was this because of her uncle? Her heart hurt to think that Westley still believed he'd somehow failed by letting her uncle get so close. "This mess with my uncle was not your fault." She implored him to understand. "You have to accept that. There was no way for you or anyone to suspect Uncle Patrick killed my father and was the one trying to kill me."

A tender smile played at the corner of his mouth. "I do know that. I just wish I'd caught him sooner so you wouldn't have had to go through all of this."

"I'm okay and he's in custody. He won't hurt me again, not from prison."

A pang of sadness for her mom thrummed through Felicity. The conversations Felicity and her mother had had over the past few hours had been tense and tearful, but better than any conversations they'd had before. Felicity felt they'd turned a corner in their relationship. Her mom had asked if Felicity would come to San Francisco for Christmas this year. She'd agreed.

"Boyd Sullivan is still out there." Westley stepped back, putting distance between them. "You're still a target. You need protection 24/7. I can't provide that for you anymore."

She stepped toward him. "Why? Why can't you?"

He spread his hands wide, as if encompassing the obviousness of it all. "We will have to work together again one day. I'm not going to risk your career because I can't control my feelings for you."

Her heart skipped a little bit. He *did* care for her. A smile spread through her, from the top of her head to the tips of her toes. "You *do* have feelings for me," she nearly whispered.

He ran a hand through his hair. "Of course I do, Felicity," he huffed. "But if I stay close to you…"

Her mouth went dry. "Westley."

He took another step back. "I will not act on my feelings. There's too much at stake. Your career. My career."

Her heart beat hard in her throat. She moved a step closer. "What if I told you I have feelings for you, too?"

He held up a hand as if to ward her off. "No, no. We can't go down that road."

"But what if I want to?" She made up the distance with two steps. He stepped back again. This dance was taking them across the room toward the door. She frowned. "What are you afraid of, Westley?"

"I can never be the man you need." The words were harsh, as if torn from him.

Absorbing his statement, she shook her head, denying his claim. "Of course you are. Don't you understand? I'm in love with you, Westley."

The color drained from his face. "You can't be."

"But I am and you're going have to face the fact that you love me, too." She prayed her words were true as she stepped closer and grasped the sleeve of his jacket. The cotton fabric was soft and crumbled easily beneath her fingers. The man wearing it was the polar opposite. "Do you deny loving me?"

His gaze fixated on her hand then rose to meet hers. There was so much torment in his eyes that she hurt for him. And she hurt for herself, because she knew he would never own up to his feelings for her. She just didn't understand why.

He gently pried her fingers loose and held her hands in his. "Felicity, I care for you more than I've ever cared for anyone else."

That gave her a spurt of hope.

"But the United States Air Force is our lives. Our careers. I will not allow anything to derail your career."

"That's not your choice to make."

He let go of her hand and took two steps back this time. His hand grasped onto the doorknob. "I'll talk to Lieutenant General Hall. I'll have Caleb and maybe Ethan and Linc, or whoever else I can get from Security Forces to rotate in."

Her fingers curled into her palms. He wasn't giving her a chance to choose for herself.

"I'm not saying I won't be there for you, Felicity. I will, but I just can't do it around-the-clock. It's too painful."

He opened the door and gave her one last longing look that broke her heart in two. "I'm sorry."

Motioning to Dakota, he said, "Stay. Guard." Then Westley disappeared out the door.

Felicity staggered to the desk and sank onto the chair. What just happened? He didn't give them a chance. He didn't give her a chance to tell him that she'd... That she'd what? What she would do for them?

She looked around the photo lab, taking in the pictures hanging on the walls that she'd shot over the last week, and realized with certainty she enjoyed this job and would gladly stay in it, if that meant she and Westley could be together.

But obviously he didn't want her to be with him. Or maybe he did, but he was too scared. Either way, the outcome was the same. He'd walked away from her. From them.

A little voice inside her challenged, *What are you going to do about it, Felicity?*

She rose and walked to the window to stare out at the late April morning enveloping Canyon Air Force Base in a warm glow. She contemplated the question.

What could she do? She'd told him she loved him and he still left. Did she chase after him like some crazy stalker?

No. He didn't want her.

She would just have to learn to live without him.

FOURTEEN

Westley stared into the depths of his root-beer bottle. Around him conversation and laughter abounded through Canyon Air Force Base's popular diner. He sat at the counter because the thought of a table for one didn't appeal.

He ached from head to toe. Not from physical exertion, though he'd run the dogs and handlers hard the last two days in between searching for more of the missing dogs. No, he hurt because he missed Felicity and Dakota.

Lieutenant General Hall had agreed to let Westley rotate out of Felicity's detail and leave Dakota in place for her security.

Knowing Dakota was keeping watch over Felicity gave Westley some comfort, but he missed her laughter and the joy on her face as she captured images with her camera. And while he hated for her to experience it, he also missed the sorrow that at times darkened her eyes when she didn't think he noticed.

He noticed everything about her. And loved everything about her.

I'm in love with you, Westley.

Her words were sweet torment.

But it was for the best that he kept a distance between them, for both of their sakes. And if he kept reminding himself of that fact, at some point it had to become true, right?

A hand slapped him on the back of the shoulder. "Drowning your sorrows there, Westley?"

Westley slanted a glance sidewise to see Special Agent Ian Steffen sliding onto the stool next to him. He sat up straight. "No, sir." He winced. "I mean, yes, sir."

Ian waved off the formality. "Relax. We're just two guys sitting at a counter having a soda." Ian gave the amber bottle nestled in Westley's hand a once-over. "Root beer. Okay. I'll take one of those," he told the waitress who came over. She nodded, grabbed a bottle from refrigerator, popped off the top and plunked it down on the counter in front of Ian before walking away.

Westley sank back into his dejected mode. Funny how easy it was. He'd thought he'd long ago shaken off feeling sorry for himself, but without Felicity in his life, he felt lost and adrift. The future he'd once seen so clearly had dissolved into mist. He didn't know what to do now. It all seemed so bleak.

"Cyberintelligence cracked the pass code on the folder in Graham's tablet," Ian told him.

Westley gave the man his attention. "And?"

"As we thought, it contained all of Graham's case notes on the hit-and-run, including incriminating evidence against his brother-in-law," Ian replied. "Not that we need the evidence with all that transpired."

"But at least we know for sure," Westley said. He peeled at the label of the root beer bottle. He was glad for Felicity's sake that she had closure on her father's death.

After a beat of silence, Ian asked, "What ails you?"

Westley shrugged. "It's been a long week." Actually a long few days. Days without Felicity in his life.

"You want to tell me why you asked to be rotated off Staff Sergeant Monroe's protection detail?"

Should he confess to the OSI agent that he'd grown fond...no, *fond* wasn't the right word. Grown to *love* his charge?

If he did, there would be no going back.

"Personal reasons," he finally said. He wouldn't put either of their careers, especially Felicity's, in jeopardy.

Ian gave him a dubious look. "Right. I think you've fallen in love with the pretty staff sergeant and are afraid to do anything about it."

Westley choked on a sip of root beer. He cleared his throat and took probably one of the biggest gambles of his career by looking the agent in the eye. "Excuse me?"

Ian grinned. "Man, it's obvious." His dark eyes actually twinkled with certainty. Westley couldn't decide if the roiling in his stomach came from relief or terror. "I remember that feeling from long ago when I first met my late wife."

"Do you regret falling in love?" Westley asked. The thought of losing Felicity terrified him. But so did living without her. He couldn't win.

It was Ian's turn to stare into the abyss of his root-beer bottle. "I learned along the way that regret only breeds discontentment. You do what you do, with the most information you have at the time, and sometimes it works great." He lifted a muscular shoulder. "Sometimes not so much, but at least you did something." He stared Westley in the eyes. "Running away isn't doing something. It's chickening out. Running away is not what we do in the US Air Force."

Westley straightened. "I'm not running away."

"Looks that way to me."

"I don't want to do anything to jeopardize her career. She wants to be a dog trainer. We can't be in the same chain of command."

Ian arched an eyebrow. "You could move over to Security Forces and be a dog handler. You could leave the service and go into civilian law enforcement."

Westley had thought of those same options. "I don't know what would be the right decision." He blew out a breath and pushed back against the counter. "Frankly, I don't feel worthy of her love."

Ian shook his head. "I never pegged you as insecure. Get over yourself. Does she love you?"

A tremble coursed through Westley. "She said she did."

The man scoffed. "What are you sitting here for? That's where you start," Ian insisted. "All the rest of the decisions will work themselves out."

Could it be that simple? "I wish her father was here so I can ask for her hand, because he would either give me his blessing or tell me to get lost."

"Still sounds vaguely to me like you're looking for another excuse to bolt. But that's just me." Ian shrugged.

Westley shook his head. "Agent Steffen, don't go easy on me, or anything—"

"Okay, okay." Ian laughed, holding up his hands in mock surrender. "Just saying…" He trailed off, then eyed Westley speculatively. "She has a mother, you know."

"Yes, yes, she does."

"Colleen Monroe is a tough and shrewd woman. If you can obtain her blessing then you're set."

Westley swigged the last of his root beer and contemplated everything the agent had said. He did need to get over himself. Felicity loved him despite his family history. He'd left his parents' failings behind when he joined the air force.

Of the options available to him, he realized it didn't matter what he did. The only option he couldn't live with was not having Felicity in his life. "You're right, Agent Steffen," he said with determination. "I need to go after what I want."

He wanted Felicity in his life as surely as she was in his heart.

Ian tipped his root beer bottle toward Westley's. Westley clinked his bottle against Ian's.

"Here's to going after what you want," the agent said.

"Aim high—" Westley began the USAF motto.

"Fly, fight, win," Ian said, finishing his sentence.

Sliding off the bar stool, Westley said, "I'd better go make a phone call."

With a nod of thanks, Westley headed out the door with purpose in his stride.

Felicity arrived home three nights later, escorted by one of the base MPs and with Dakota trotting alongside her. The dog had been her constant companion even as the detail changed every eight hours. Westley had been true to his word that she would be protected around-the-clock. She was grateful. She really was, but she missed him. Missed the way his eyes crinkled at the corners when he was amused. Missed the way he made her feel safe and cherished.

Shoulders slumped, she was headed up the walkway toward her front door when Heidi stepped out of the house next door and called her name.

Needing a friend right now, Felicity hesitated. Many people on base believed the reporter to be the anonymous blogger leaking information to the public. Could Felicity trust her?

Only one way to find out. Felicity did an about-face and moved past the guard. Dakota stayed right at her heels. She met Heidi at the shared property line.

"Hi, Heidi. How are you tonight?" Felicity asked, careful to keep the despair she clinging to her from tingeing her voice.

"Better than you, I take it," Heidi said. "You look like somebody kicked your dog." Heidi smiled at Dakota. "But he looks okay."

That's kind of how Felicity felt. Except Dakota was right here, healthy and strong and willing to protect her even when Westley wasn't willing.

Her hands tangled in Dakota's fur. She dredged up a smile for Heidi. "I'm okay. Still trying to process everything."

"I'm so sorry about your uncle," Heidi said.

"Thanks. Me, too."

Heidi glanced toward the security guard. "I thought Westley was detailed to your protection."

"He needed to do some things at the training center," Felicity said. The ache in her chest intensified. "He'll rotate back in at some point." At least she hoped so. Then they could talk and resolve some of their issues. Or not. It had been three days since he walked out of her office in the photo lab. Three days with strangers following her around base, sleeping on her couch, watching out for Boyd Sullivan. Three days with her wishing Westley was there beside her. Only the presence of Dakota brought her any peace.

Depression and exhaustion set in. "I need to go get some rest," she told Heidi. "We have new recruits coming in tomorrow and I want to catch them as they get off the bus."

Heidi smiled gently. "Sure, no problem. I'll talk to you later."

"Thanks." Felicity hurried into the house, the young guard following her. "Make yourself at home," she told the MP.

She went to the refrigerator and grabbed herself a ginger ale to settle her upset stomach. Then she and Dakota headed upstairs. He was the only one she let witness her tears.

"Master Sergeant James, what can I do for you?" The clipped female voice on the other end of the phone line had Westley straightening his spine and squaring his shoulders. He stared out the window of his small studio apartment in base housing. From this vantage point he could see the parade grounds, where several vintage planes were on display, a sight he never tired of.

Taking a breath and gathering his courage, he said, "I am calling to ask for your permission to marry your daughter."

Colleen Monroe's voice dipped. "Excuse me? You want to marry Felicity?"

Though they were miles apart and he couldn't see

her, he recognized the strength in her voice. This was a woman used to intimidating others.

"Yes, ma'am, I do. I'm in love with your daughter."

After a heartbeat of silence, she asked, "How well do you know my daughter?"

"I know her very well. We are stationed together at Canyon Air Force Base."

"I owe you a debt of gratitude, Master Sergeant James," the woman said, her tone soft with emotion. "Felicity told me how you saved her life on several occasions. You have my permission to ask her to marry you." There was a smile in her voice.

Tension drained from his shoulders. "Thank you."

Now to convince Felicity to give him another chance.

Felicity hurried down the hall toward Lieutenant General Hall's office. She'd been summoned a few minutes ago from the photo lab, where she was busy uploading today's photos to the FBI database. Thus far she hadn't captured any images of Boyd Sullivan.

She knocked on the lieutenant general's door and heard a male voice say "Enter."

Pushing open the door, she stepped inside and froze. Lieutenant General Hall sat behind his desk, but it was the sight of Westley standing in front of the desk that made her pulse race. She drank up the sight of him. He wore his semiformal dress uniform, the dark navy coat looking sharp over his broad shoulders and tapered waist. His creased navy pants and black shoes made him appear taller. Formidable.

The moment his tender gaze met hers, her mouth dried like the desert.

"Come all the way in, Staff Sergeant," Lieutenant General Hall instructed.

Buying herself time to process the situation, she closed the door, adjusted her uniform coat and patted her braided hair before turning back around and walking slowly toward the two men.

She drew herself to attention and trained her focus on the lieutenant general. She saluted. "Sir?"

"At ease," Lieutenant General Hall said. He stood. "I'll give you two the room."

"Sir?" Confusion ran rampant through her system.

Lieutenant General Hall rounded the desk and stopped beside her. He put his hand on her shoulder. "Your father would be proud of you, Felicity."

Her mouth dropped open as the lieutenant general left the room. Then her gaze sought Westley's. "I don't understand."

He stepped close and took her hands in his. "I can explain but first I want to know if you'll give me another chance."

She inhaled sharply. "Are you ready to give us a chance?"

"I am," he said. "You were right. I was afraid. Afraid of failing you or disappointing you."

Tenderness filled her.

"But as someone recently told me, I need to get over myself and go after what I want."

"What is it you want?"

"You. Us." He lifted her hands to his lips and kissed her knuckles. "I love you, Felicity. I want to spend the rest of my life making you happy. Keeping you safe. Loving you."

Her breath held in her lungs. Excitement bubbled inside her chest. "What are you asking me, Westley?"

"Will you marry me?"

Elation engulfed her, making her head swim. "Yes. Yes, I'll marry you."

He let out a shout of joy and clasped his arms around her and swung her off her feet into a dizzying circle. When her feet touched the ground she leaned toward him, needing a kiss.

But he held back. His face was serious as he looked at her. "Are you sure?"

Was he still so unsure of her, unsure of her feelings for him?

She laid her hands on his chest, feeling his heart beating in double time. She would spend the rest of her days making sure this man knew her love was true and forever. "Yes, I am sure. I want to marry you. I want to spend the rest of my days with you and, God willing, there will be many, many days."

She fought back the specter of Boyd Sullivan and his horrible roses and notes. She wouldn't allow him and his threats to crowd in on her happiness.

A grin spread across Westley's face. "Close your eyes," he said.

"What?"

"Trust me. Close your eyes."

She closed her eyes. He wrapped an arm around her waist and turned her around. "We're walking," he said.

Chuckling, she allowed him to lead her forward. She heard the office door open. Then they were walking on the carpeted hallway toward the entrance of the building.

"How much farther?" she asked.

"Just a bit," he said. "No peeking."

"I won't." She heard the click of the outside doors opening and then they stepped out into the evening breeze.

"Stairs," he told her. He led her down the steps in front of the command building and then across the asphalt of the driveway.

Her feet sank in the grass. Overhead the flap of the American flag let her know they were standing beneath the flagpole in front of the command center. She heard a chuckle, but not from Westley.

"Don't open your eyes until I say so, okay?" Westley asked.

She sighed. "Okay, fine."

He moved away from her, leaving her standing there alone. But she wasn't afraid. She knew she was safe. Westley was close by.

"Open your eyes," he said.

She blinked against the setting sun as her eyes focused. People stood at the edges of the lawn, but it was only the two males directly in front of her that held her attention.

Dakota sat next to a kneeling Westley, a large bow decorated the German shepherd's neck. Her gaze locked on the small little silver box dangling from the ribbon. Her heart fluttered with delight.

"Surprise," Westley said.

"Is that…?" She swallowed.

Westley undid the bow, letting the little silver box drop into his open palm.

She edged closer. Her body quivered with excitement.

He opened the box and held it up for her to see a

beautiful marquis solitaire ring nestled next to a braided gold band.

"Felicity Monroe, will you please do me the honor of becoming my wife?"

She went down on her knees in front of him, her hands closing over his. "Yes. A thousand times, yes."

He slipped the diamond ring on her finger.

Dakota let out a happy *woof.* A cheer went up from the spectators. She lifted her gaze to see that so many of their friends had gathered to witness the proposal. She grinned.

Westley touched the braided ring still nestled in the box. "This is for the ceremony and for you to wear whenever you don't want to wear the diamond. It's not safe to wear the diamond when you're working with dogs."

One of the issues they needed to resolve. She closed the box. "I'm the base photographer."

"Only until the Red Rose Killer is caught."

"What happens after that?"

"Once you are no longer in danger, I will give up my post and go into civilian law enforcement."

She shook head. "Unacceptable. The only way this will work is if you stay at the training center."

He opened his mouth to argue, but she put a finger to his lips. "Don't you see? This way I get the best of both worlds. You stay at the training center and I can come visit you and the dogs anytime I want. You do your dream job and I get to be a photographer. A dream I never even realized I wanted."

His lips split in a broad grin. "I love you."

"Good. I'll need to hear that a lot." She held up her hand, admiring the sparkly ring on her finger. "I will wear this diamond with pride and joy. But more importantly, I will love you for always."

He cupped her head and kissed her. Another cheer went up. Dakota wedged his way between them, breaking the kiss. The dog licked her face. She and Westley laughed with happiness. And they would be happy. Despite Boyd, despite her uncle and despite any threat to try to come between them.

Westley helped her to her feet. "How soon should we do this?"

"As soon as Pastor Harmon is available," she said.

Westley waggled his eyebrows. "I was hoping you'd say that. We have him booked for tomorrow afternoon."

She giggled. "You don't waste any time."

"I don't want to spend another moment without you by my side."

"By your side is where I want to be. Always."

"It's been a month, people," Lieutenant General Hall said as he stood at the head of the conference table. Concern and displeasure were etched in his face, causing tension to ripple through the room.

Westley exchanged a quick glance with Felicity. His wife. Joy filled his heart. He took her hand beneath the table. They could face anything together.

They'd married in an intimate ceremony at the Christian church on base with Pastor Harmon officiating. Felicity's mother had flown in and Ian had walked the bride down the aisle. Lieutenant General Hall had stood up as Westley's best man, while Felicity's friend Rae Fallon had been her maid of honor.

Westley and Felicity decided to postpone a formal honeymoon until after all the dogs were safely returned and Boyd Sullivan imprisoned once again. Westley moved his belonging from his studio apartment to Felicity's house. He'd thought it would feel odd to live in the home she's shared with her father but it wasn't at all. In fact, he wanted to believe that Graham Monroe would have approved.

Felicity continued on as the base photographer, and Westley, with Dakota by his side, kept her safe 24/7. He still kept tabs on the training center, though Master Sergeant Caleb Streeter was in command. And he still worked to find the dogs that remained missing. Thirty-two dogs were still unaccounted for, including the prized four German shepherds. Searching for the dogs and protecting Felicity kept him busy. Guarding Felicity around the clock brought him immense joy marred only by the anxiety of the missing dogs.

This morning, Lieutenant General Hall had called this meeting out of well-known frustration. Boyd Sullivan was still at large. And the identity of his accomplice, someone here on base, remained a mystery.

"Special Agent Davison," Lieutenant General Hall said as he turned to the man on his right. "Please update us on the Red Rose Killer."

FBI Special Agent Oliver Davison stood to address the room. "We have conflicting reports all over the state of sightings of Boyd Sullivan. Now we're getting reports of him being as far away as Louisiana."

A murmur went through the room.

Lieutenant General Hall pinned his gaze on Captain Justin Blackwood. "And his accomplice?"

Justin planted his hands on the table and said, "We are doing our best to find the person who helped Boyd gain access to the base, sir."

Lieutenant General Hall's jaw tightened. "Someone had to have seen something or knows something." His gaze swept the room, landing briefly on each Security Forces member present. "I want answers, people. I want the base turned inside out and upside down if need be."

Everyone nodded.

One of the Security Forces members, Lieutenant Preston Flanigan, spoke up. "I still say Zoe Sullivan, Boyd's half sister, is his accomplice."

Tech Sergeant Linc Colson leaned forward to stare at the other man. "I'm on it," he said in a warning tone that left no doubt he was telling the other MP to back off. "If Zoe is his accomplice I will find out."

Lieutenant General Hall nodded his approval. "All right, then. Dismissed."

Westley and Felicity filed out with everyone else.

"I need to grab my camera," she said.

They linked fingers and headed to the photo lab. Once inside he shut the door and took her fully into his arms.

"Another day in paradise," he said with a smile.

She wound her arms around his neck and pulled him closer. "Every day is paradise with you. And I know here, in your arms, I'll always be safe."

"On my watch. Always."

And she kissed him.

* * * * *

The hunt for the Red Rose Killer continues.
Look for the next exciting stories
in the MILITARY K-9 UNIT *series.*

MISSION TO PROTECT
—Terri Reed, April 2018

BOUND BY DUTY
—Valerie Hansen, May 2018

TOP SECRET TARGET
—Dana Mentink, June 2018

STANDING FAST
—Maggie K. Black, July 2018

RESCUE OPERATION
—Lenora Worth, August 2018

EXPLOSIVE FORCE
—Lynette Eason, September 2018

BATTLE TESTED
—Laura Scott, October 2018

VALIANT DEFENDER
—Shirlee McCoy, November 2018

MILITARY K-9 UNIT CHRISTMAS
—Valerie Hansen and Laura Scott, December 2018

Dear Reader

I hope you have enjoyed the first book in the Military K-9 Unit continuity series. When I was asked to be a part of this editor-created project, I was elated and nervous. This is my first foray into writing about military heroes, both two-legged and four. I have the utmost respect and admiration for our military-service women and men. In writing this novel, I called upon many experts and ex-military personnel for help and guidance. Please forgive any and all mistakes as some creative license was taken for the sake of the story.

Developing the characters of Westley and Felicity was both fun and challenging. I needed them to be strong, honorable and brave, but vulnerable enough to let down the walls around their hearts and fall in love. Each came to the story with old wounds that needed to be healed before they could find their happy ending. Westley was afraid he would repeat the patterns of behavior modeled to him by his parents. And Felicity battled with insecurity, which kept her from permitting anyone to get close. But love softened their hearts and allowed them both to be open to a future together.

Through the next seven books you will find more stories of romance and mystery as the men and women of the fictional Canyon Air Force Base fall in love and bring down the Red Rose Killer. Enjoy!

Blessings,
Terri Reed

Get 2 Free Books,
Plus 2 Free Gifts—
just for trying the
Reader Service!

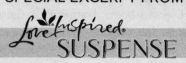
She was being watched. Constantly. Every fiber of her
being knew it. Lately she felt as though she was the
defenseless prey and packs of predators were circling
her and her helpless little boy, which was why she'd left
Freddy home with a sitter. Were things as bad as they
seemed? It was more than possible, and Staff Sergeant Zoe
Sullivan shivered despite the warm spring day.

Scanning the busy parking lot as she left the Canyon
Air Force Base Exchange with her purchases, Zoe quickly
spotted one of the Security Forces investigators. Her pulse
jumped, and hostility took over her usually amiable spirit.
The K-9 cop in a blue beret and camo ABU—Airman
Battle Uniform—was obviously waiting for her. She bit
her lip. Nobody cared how innocent she was. Being the
half sister of Boyd Sullivan, the escaped Red Rose Killer,
automatically made her a person of interest.

Zoe clenched her teeth. There was no way she could prove herself so why bother trying? She squared her slim shoulders under her off-duty blue T-shirt and stepped out, heading straight for the Security Forces man and his imposing K-9, a black-and-rust-colored rottweiler.

Clearly he saw her coming because he tensed, feet apart, body braced. In Zoe's case, five and a half feet was the most height she could muster. The dark-haired tech sergeant she was approaching looked to be almost a foot taller.

He gave a slight nod as she drew near and greeted her formally. "Sergeant Sullivan."

Linc Colson's firm jaw, broad shoulders and strength of presence were familiar. They had met during a questioning session conducted by Captain Justin Blackwood and Master Sergeant Westley James shortly after her half brother had escaped from prison.

Zoe stopped and gave the cop an overt once-over, checking his name tag. "Can I help you with something, Sergeant Colson?"

Don't miss
BOUND BY DUTY by Valerie Hansen,
available May 2018 wherever
Love Inspired® Suspense books and ebooks are sold.

www.LoveInspired.com

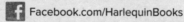

Love Inspired®

Inspirational Romance to Warm Your Heart and Soul

Join our social communities to connect with other readers who share your love!

Sign up for the Love Inspired newsletter at **www.LoveInspired.com** to be the first to find out about upcoming titles, special promotions and exclusive content.

CONNECT WITH US AT:

Harlequin.com/Community

 Facebook.com/LoveInspiredBooks

 Twitter.com/LoveInspiredBks

LISOCIAL2017